OUTLAW'S EMPIRE

OUTLAW'S EMPIRE

RAY HOGAN

DOUBLEDAY & COMPANY, INC.
GARDEN CITY, NEW YORK
1986

All the characters in this book
are fictitious, and any resemblance
to actual persons, living or dead,
is purely coincidental.

Library of Congress Cataloging-on-Publication Data
Hogan, Ray, 1908–
Outlaw's empire.
I. Title.
PS3558.0347309 1986   813'.54   85-13082
ISBN: 0-385-23254-3

for my wife, LOIS

OUTLAW'S EMPIRE

1

Riley Tabor drew up short as he walked along the hallway of the Buffalo City Hotel. The crash of furniture, the clatter of breaking glass and loud cursing and grunting could mean only one thing; there was a hell of a fight going on in Room 5 just ahead. Tabor shrugged, resumed his way down the dark, narrow corridor. A man bedding down in one of Dodge City's flop joints had to expect things like that.

Abruptly the door of Number 5 flew open. A woman, only partly dressed, long hair streaming about her bare shoulders, face a chalk mask of terror, burst into the hallway.

"They—they're killing him!" she gasped, clutching clothing to her body with one hand while she seized Riley's wrist with the other. "Help him—please!"

Tabor frowned, hesitated. A tall, well-muscled cowhand with dark hair and eyes, he well knew the old adage of never mixing into another man's quarrel—especially when there was a woman involved.

"Hurry—please!" the woman pleaded. "There's three of them—and he's not like them! He's from back east and they're all—"

Tabor took a long step forward, and gun in hand headed for the open doorway. It sounded as if some hardcases had cornered a greenhorn and were out to take his life for one reason or another. It could be over the woman, an attractive, honey-haired blonde, or maybe it was just another holdup. There was a lot of that going on around Dodge, so much so that there was talk of passing a law forbidding the carrying of firearms.

The room was poorly lit by a single lamp, the late afternoon sunlight being shut out by a shade drawn over the solitary window. Riley, stepping quickly inside the musty cubicle, saw that two of the men, ordinary-looking cowhands, had pinned the struggling easterner, also just partly dressed, to the floor. One was sitting on his legs, the other on his arms, which were extended above his head. The third man—a rancher, at first glance—was crouched over the intended victim, one hand clamped over the man's mouth to stifle any outcry, the other gripping a long-bladed knife.

"Back off!" Riley shouted, working deeper into the littered room.

He had recognized the easterner as a man he had talked to in the Long Branch Saloon the day before. His name was Adam Hale. He had a team and wagon and was heading west. Riley, out of a job at the end of a trail drive, with only his gear and no horse, was looking for a ride back to New Mexico. Someone had mentioned that Hale was going in that direction, but when Riley approached him the easterner had turned him down.

"Who the hell are you?" the man with the knife snarled, looking up. He had a large, florid face surrounded by a thick shock of black hair and a heavy beard.

"I'm the one with a gun in my hand!" Tabor snapped. "Telling you again—drop that knife!"

"I ain't about to! I'm going to geld this sonofabitch. That was my woman he had in here and I aim to fix him so's he won't ever bother no other man's wife!"

At that moment Hale jerked an arm free and lashed out

at the man with the blade. The blow knocked him back against the wall. Hale, kicking free of the one imprisoning his legs, and wrenching his other arm clear, rolled to one side.

"You ain't getting away from me!"

The knife glittered in the muted light as the man holding it lunged for the easterner. Riley fired. The bullet struck the man in the shoulder, the force of the heavy .45 slug rocking him to one side. He began to yell and curse as smoke gathered suddenly in the hot, motionless air of the room.

"Shoot him, Guzman! Shoot that—"

Guzman, the nearest of the pair who had been holding Hale to the floor, twisted about, leveled pistol in his hand. Tabor triggered his weapon again. Guzman, on his knees, went over backward, a broad stain spreading across his chest.

"Damn it, Jude—shoot! Shoot!"

Jude, the second of the cowhands, shook his head and raised his hands. "He's done killed Guzman, Mr. Madden. I sure ain't asking for the same thing!"

Riley Tabor backed quickly to the door and glanced out into the hallway. The woman had disappeared, and there was no one else in the corridor. There was a chance the gunshots had gone unnoticed—but only a chance.

"Get your clothes on!" he snapped angrily at Hale, reentering the room and closing the door. He had just killed a man—a stranger—as a result of sticking his nose into someone else's business. "And you," he added to Jude. "Keep on reaching."

Shifting his glance to Madden, he gestured warningly with his gun and took up a stand just to the left of the door, where he would be in position to act should anyone come to investigate.

He was through in Dodge now for sure. He had no choice other than to leave, even if it meant buying a ticket on the stagecoach from his sorely depleted wages. But he reckoned that was all right. He'd hung around town for a week or better, and now that he'd had his fill of easy living—whiskey, women and gambling—it was high time he got back to New Mexico and rustled himself up a job.

"You got no business horning in on something that ain't none of your butt-in, mister!" Madden said, one hand clamped to his bleeding shoulder. "I sure ain't going to forget it."

"It's best you do," Tabor replied coolly. "Far as me butting in—I didn't like the odds—three to one."

"That's the kind he's got coming! Was my woman he talked into coming up here. It's sure my right to do what I want with him!"

"Maybe—if you'd taken him on alone, man to man, with your fists or your gun—and not with all that help—"

Hale, dressed, had circled the clutter in the center of the room and moved to Riley's side. "The lady was more than willing," he said, breaking into the conversation. "Perhaps if you had paid a little more attention to her and a little less to raising cows we wouldn't all be here now."

Tabor had returned to the door as Hale spoke, and laying a hand on the black iron thumb latch he opened the flimsy panel. Again he glanced up and down the hallway. Empty. Luck was still with them.

"Got to gag and tie them," he said, turning back to Hale. "We'll need time to get out of here."

Adam Hale nodded, and crossing to the bed jerked off the blanket and ripped it into several strips. While Tabor continued to stand guard at the door, he relieved Madden and Jude of their weapons, tossed them into a far corner, and after binding their hands behind them drew a strip of the cloth tightly over their mouths. Madden, despite his wound, put up considerable opposition, but Hale, a tall, well-built man, handled him with ease.

"How bad's he hurt?" Riley asked as Hale rejoined him.

"He won't bleed to death if that's what you mean," the easterner replied bluntly. "Anyway, they'll work themselves loose after a bit."

With Hale following, Tabor hurried out into the hall and closed the door. Immediately they could hear the two men inside begin to thresh about.

"I've got a friend over on the other side of the tracks who'll hide us out for a spell," Riley said, reloading. Hale, he noted, did not carry a gun. "We can go there."

"Not necessary," Hale cut in, his words clipped and businesslike. "My rig's all ready to move out. Had intended to leave right after noon. Got things all set—then I ran into the lady. Horses and wagon are waiting at the livery stable." The easterner paused, thrust out his hand to Tabor. "I'm obliged to you for stepping in when you did. That lunatic— he really had me in tight."

Riley studied Hale, a hard smile on his lips. "You change your mind about giving me a ride west?"

Hale, showing some effect from the brawl, trim and impressive-looking in a corduroy suit, polished low-heel boots, light-colored, flat-crowned hat and yellow shirt, his black, carefully trimmed mustache and beard contrasting against the tan of his skin, shrugged.

"Was a big favor—your pitching in and helping me when you did," he said. "And I always repay a favor. That lunatic really had me in a tight . . . You have any belongings you want to pick up?"

"My saddle, slicker—some other stuff. All in my room—"

Riley broke off abruptly as a loud yell came from Number 5.

"Damn!" Hale muttered. "One of them has slipped his gag. Get your gear and let's—"

"No time left," Riley cut in, heading down the hallway at a run for its rear door. "That yelling'll bring somebody up here in a hurry. We've got to get out of town—fast!"

2

They reached the hotel's exit and broke out into the hardpack at its rear. There was no one in sight in the fading day, but from the street in front of the building they could hear men yelling back and forth.

"Your rig—which stable?" Riley asked without turning to Hale.

"Austin's. Just down the street a piece."

Tabor nodded, quickened his step. "We can get there from the alley," he said, and hurried on.

Reaching the narrow, littered alleyway behind a line of shacks and secondary buildings, they again broke into a run, paying no mind to the three or four men who paused to glance at them as they rushed along through the late afternoon shadows until they had reached the broad, tin-roofed structure that housed the livery barn.

"My wagon's in the yard on the other side," Hale said. Dark bruises were now beginning to appear on the easterner's face, and there was a streak of blood at a corner of his mouth where a lip had been crushed during the encounter with Madden and his two hired men. "We can cut through the barn."

Hale moved out ahead, reaching in his pocket as he did for a leather billfold from which he extracted a five-dollar bill.

"Paid the hostler for my rig's keep," he said. "Maybe I

can pay him again to keep quiet if anybody asks about me
. . . Here we are."

Riley looked beyond Hale. The easterner's vehicle was
one of the finest he had ever seen. It had the appearance of
an army wagon, being painted blue and red with black iron
fittings, but with many refinements. The vehicle itself was
larger; the arching canvas canopy was brown instead of
white and looked to be of much heavier material, while a
great deal of equipment was mounted along the sides of the
wagon. The team pulling it was a pair of bay geldings that
reminded Riley of some workhorses he had once seen—
Belgians, he thought they were called—only these animals
were somewhat smaller.

"Mighty fine outfit," he remarked as they hurried toward
the rig.

"Ought to be," Hale replied. "Had it built special—oak
frame and box, heavier hickory spoke wheels and wider
rims, and gumwood axles. The Studebaker company put it
together for me at my specific instructions."

Both men were breathing hard from the fast pace they
had maintained since leaving the Buffalo City Hotel, and
twice Hale paused in his speaking for breath.

"Get the tie rope," he said as they drew alongside the
wagon. He turned, glanced toward the barn as the sound of
running footsteps reached them. "It's the hostler," he said,
relief in his voice.

Riley, jerking the slip-knotted rope free of the post to
which it had been tied, quickly secured it to a ring in the
near horse's collar, and climbed up beside Hale, already
settled on the seat.

"Want you to have this," the easterner called down to the
hostler, a grinning young man in stained overalls.

"But you done paid—"

"Paid for stabling my horses and looking after my wagon. This is for keeping your mouth shut if anybody comes looking for me—"

The hostler blinked. "Looking for you—you mean maybe the law?"

"Maybe—"

The stablehand shook his head. "Well, now, I ain't so sure about mixing up in your trouble," he said hesitantly.

Hale extracted another five dollars from his billfold and tossed it to the man. "Expect this will help you forget all about me," he said, and taking up the reins kicked off the break and started the horses moving.

"Yeh—reckon it sure will!" the hostler called. "Which way you heading?"

"North," Riley shouted before Hale could make a reply. Leaning back in the padded seat, he threw his glance in the direction of the street beyond Austin's. There seemed to be considerable activity in the area of the Buffalo City Hotel. Evidently Madden and Jude had been able to attract attention and were now free. Hale was aware of the probability; he had whipped up his team and they were now moving rapidly away from the settlement.

"Which road you aiming to take?" Riley asked.

"Cimarron Cutoff," Adam replied. "Was told to take the road along the river and I'd come to it."

Tabor nodded. He had traveled through the area, both the Cimarron and the Mountain routes, a dozen times, and knew both well.

"How far is it to the forks?" Hale asked.

"Eighteen miles or so," Riley replied, looking back over his shoulder. No riders in sight; but if Madden had got word to Dodge City's lawmen, it was a safe bet a posse led by one of the town's marshals would soon be under way.

"Whereabouts in New Mexico are you headed?" Riley said then, satisfied no pursuit had begun yet.

"Not sure where—maybe I'll go on to Arizona," Hale said, cocking a foot on the brake pedal. Drawing a leather cigar case from the inside pocket of his coat, he offered one of the weeds to Tabor and then selected one for himself. "I'll make up my mind later on."

Riley struck a match, held it to the tip of Hale's stogie and then puffed his own into life as the wagon raced on.

"Good country—New Mexico," he said.

The span of bays were moving along at a fast trot, and at their present rate of speed they would reach the forks, and the cutoff in another hour or so. Riley was breathing a little easier. If a posse did get on their trail and if darkness closed in soon, the lawmen would not be certain if the men they were after had taken the Cimarron route or stayed on the Mountain road.

"That's what I'm looking for—good country. Plan to invest in land," Hale said, pushing his hat to the back of his head and blowing a cloud of smoke into the air. The pale vapor was immediately caught up and swept into the canopied area of the wagon—loaded with bedding, boxes, a trunk, tools and other necessary items.

"Thought maybe you figured to go into ranching. If so I aimed to hit you up for a job."

Hale shook his head. "I'm a lawyer—doubt if I'd do very well as a rancher. I'm from back east—Pennsylvania, in fact. I don't suppose you've ever been there."

"No—heard of it, that's all. Seems a far piece away for a man to drive by himself—"

"Had a partner—or maybe I'd best just call him a driver. Lost him."

"Lost?" Riley repeated, once again looking back over the

road behind them. It was still devoid of riders, and darkness and the cutoff were not far off.

"Drowned, or maybe killed. We were fording a river up in Ohio. Don't know the name of it. He was out wading ahead of the horses, sort of being certain of the depth. He fell. I don't know why. Could have stepped in a hole, or maybe stumbled. I guess he hit his head on something. Next thing I knew the off horse had stepped on him. When I finally got the rig to solid ground and fished him out, he was dead. Was sorry about it but there wasn't anything I could do . . . You think my team will have any trouble making it through desert country?"

"Good stock. Don't see why they won't."

"Talked to quite a few men who know about such things back home. Some recommended mules, others oxen. I chose the bays because I was in something of a hurry. You think I was wrong?"

"Mules are fast, too, and they can go longer without water, but they've got a small hoof. They have a hell of a hard time in loose sand or snow—or mud. Oxen are fine. Most folks making the trip out here use them. Tough, and they've got a big hoof, but they're slow."

"Reason I elected not to use them. These horses of mine have a big hoof."

"Noticed that. You won't have any trouble in the sand you'll be crossing, and they ought to be able to handle any of the hills." The team, having followed a pattern of alternately a fast trot and a steady lope, had settled down to the former.

"Glad to hear that," Hale said, again exhaling a puff of smoke while his eyes fixed on a wedge of geese, like a wavering arrowhead, cutting its way north through the darkening sky.

"We going to reach the cutoff soon?"

At the easterner's question, Riley looked ahead, and then back over his shoulder. There was no sign of a posse yet. It could be that Madden had chosen not to bring in the law.

"Be there pretty quick—and I don't think there's anybody on our trail yet."

"Good thing we got out of that town fast . . . You always been a ranch hand?"

"Ever since I was big enough to sit a horse," Tabor replied. "Don't know anything else."

"Probably the best way a man can be. A jack-of-all-trades never gets far. There big money in raising cattle?"

Riley Tabor was silent as the wagon hurried on. Now and then pans clattered noisily in the back and somewhere outside the bed a chain had come loose and was clinking musically.

"Reckon so, if things go right," he said, finally. "A man's always up against the weather—sometimes a drought, other times a blizzard—or maybe a range fire. Any of those things can wipe you out—not to mention rustlers and a disease of some kind."

"Like farming," Hale said, nodding. "My folks were farmers—on a grand scale, but they were up against the same things, far as weather's concerned. Always told my father he'd be better off gambling with cards than with nature."

"For a fact. That's the forks up ahead," Riley said. "Take the left-hand road." Twisting about he glanced to the east once more. His hard-planed features drew into a frown.

"Looks like dust behind us. Could be a posse."

Hale turned, looked over his shoulder. "Dust sure enough. You know this country—what's the best thing to do?"

"Be dark in another few minutes. Way I see it, the smart thing to do is pull off into those trees and lay low until we know for certain it's the posse. Then we can figure what to do."

Hale raised himself on the seat and craned his neck to see farther ahead in the gathering darkness. "Trees look about a couple of miles away. You think we can reach them in time?"

"Whip up the team and we will—"

Hale reached for the lash, jerked it from its socket and popped the length of leather sharply over the heads of the bays. The horses, startled, lunged forward in their harness instantly, and at once the wagon began to increase speed.

Shortly they were at the division of the trail and the small settlement that had sprung up there. It was almost full dark, and Riley, hoping to avoid being seen by any of the residents, directed Hale to slow the bays and as quietly as possible swing wide of the place. It cost them precious minutes, but Tabor was certain they had not been seen and there would be no report of their passing if anyone was asked by the leader of the posse.

Well away from the division in the trail, Hale again put the horses into a gallop. They reached the outgrowth at the edge of the grove. Immediately he swung the rig off onto the rutted, rocky shoulder and down across the grassy slope that lay between the road and the dark green stand of trees.

"Going to be hard to hide a rig like mine. Trees are small," Hale commented as he began to work a course into the grove.

"Mostly junipers and piñons—maybe an oak or two. None of them ever get very big out here—but they grow thick," Riley said, hanging on to the handrail of the seat as the wagon rocked and pitched in its passage over the uneven ground. "They'll cover us all right. Just keep heading straight into them."

Hale said nothing. His face was taut, and sweat laid a shine upon it as he crouched forward and sought to guide the team and wagon deeper into the trees. Finally he drew the bays to a halt.

"Far as we can go," he said, wrapping the lines about the whipstock. Reaching down under the seat and brushing aside a fold of canvas, he took out the rifle it was covering. The weapon, the latest model of the lever action type, appeared to be new.

Riley, on the ground as quickly as the vehicle had stopped, glanced up at Hale and shook his head. "You won't be needing that. If it's a posse we'll be dealing with the law," he said, and moving off a few paces turned his attention to the road. For a long minute he was motionless, intent on listening, and then he returned to the wagon.

"Made it just in time," he said to Hale. "I can hear horses —a dozen or so—coming this way. Expect somebody in Cimarron saw us go by after all—or else that hostler back in Dodge done some talking."

"He knew I aimed to take the cutoff," Hale admitted. "Was talking to him yesterday . . . About using my rifle, I appreciate your advice, but I'm in too much of a hurry to get hung up."

"First just sit quiet till we see what they do—"

"Know that pretty quick," Hale said. "I can see them through the trees from up here."

3

It was too far and too dark to tell much about the riders, Riley saw. There were ten or twelve men in the posse, and they were passing at a good lope. When the hammering of their horses' hooves had faded, he turned to Hale.

"Best we set right here. They'll be doubling back."

Shielding the flare of a match with a cupped hand, Hale relit his cigar. "They'll easy find us in here if they do any looking."

"Probably won't. Posses peter out quick when they don't have any luck first off. My guess is they'll head on back to Dodge, and start out again at daylight when they can see better."

Hale stared off into the darkness of the grove. Back in the direction of Cimarron, the settlement at the forks, a dog was barking, the sound far off and lonely.

"No point continuing on the cutoff then," the easterner said. "They know we'll be on it."

Tabor agreed. "Was wondering about that. There some reason you want to take the cutoff?"

Hale stirred indifferently. Handsome, with a strong, square-cut face, he had the easy way of a truly self-confident man.

"No, none, other than it being the shortest route."

"Smart thing for us to do then is head back to the Mountain trail, forget the cutoff."

"Sounds like a good idea. Means we'll have to cross the river, doesn't it?"

"Yeh, there's a ford a few miles on west of the forks. Can cross over there. Probably have plenty of company. Most pilgrims stay on the Mountain trail."

"They call that the Bent's Fort route too, don't they?"

"Right, but there's not much left of either one. The old fort's in ruins and the new one, well, there hasn't been anything going on there since around 'sixty. Probably a wagon trader or two living off pilgrims. Not much else along the way till we get to Trinidad."

"Having company sounds good—especially where there's women concerned," Hale said, smiling.

Tabor frowned. "A woman's what got you—us—in that fracas back in Dodge—"

Hale puffed on the butt of his cigar for several moments, and then tossed it aside.

"Was worth it. Ran into her at one of the mercantiles. Wasn't much for looks where her face was concerned, but the way she was put together made a man forget that.

"We got to talking, and like a lot of married women she wasn't having much of a life. Lonely, most of the time. Didn't take much to get her to that hotel room. We were enjoying ourselves a'plenty when her husband and those two hired hands of his showed up."

The dog was still barking, flinging his objections to the now brightly shining moon. Riley listened for a brief time and then shrugged.

"Bad business fooling around with another man's wife. You make a habit of it?"

"Every chance I get," Hale said promptly. "I believe in taking care of all women—married or single—as long as they're willing, and most are. Spent most of my early life working hard. No time for anything but work and study. Then I lost my intended wife in a fire. That changed my way of thinking. Figured life was just too uncertain, so now I pluck my roses whenever the opportunity presents itself— and so far it has been fairly often."

"That rancher back in Dodge just about ended all that for you—"

"No doubt about that, and I'll be eternally grateful to you for showing up when you did."

Riley made no comment. After a moment, he turned and walked off in the direction of the road. The night was cool and quiet, the hush broken only by the continued barking of the dog at the forks.

Tabor wasn't too pleased to be riding with a man like Adam Hale. It wasn't that Hale's apparent morals were at issue; hell, he had plenty of drawbacks himself that he reckoned other folks didn't care for, but somehow he wasn't comfortable around the man. However, he realized there was nothing he could do about it at the moment other than stay with Hale; perhaps, when they encountered a wagon train or another pilgrim on the Mountain trail, which they were certain to do, he could find someone else to ride with.

All he owned was on his back: the hasty departure from Dodge City had cost him his saddle, his extra clothing, his slicker and his blanket roll, all of which wouldn't add up to much. He had what money was left from the wages paid him at the end of the drive, in the money belt around his middle, and he had his gun. Riley reckoned he'd make out. As soon as he got to one of the big towns in New Mexico— Las Vegas or maybe Santa Fe—he'd cut loose from Hale, if he was still riding with him, and start hunting up a job.

"They're coming back—"

Adam Hale's voice reached out through the silver-shot

darkness to Riley and brought him around. Putting his attention on the road beyond the grove, he listened. At once he caught the rap of loping horses. It would be the posse. They had tired of the fruitless chase, just as he'd figured they would, and were returning to Dodge City.

"We'll give them a quarter hour or so, and then move out," Tabor said, dropping back to the wagon and climbing up onto the seat.

"Whatever you think best," Hale agreed. "You know these people so I'll leave it up to you. Still figure it best to take the Mountain trail?"

"Sure do. Nine chances out of ten the marshal at the head of the bunch will be right back here first thing in the morning with his posse. And if we do this right, he'll believe we're somewhere down the cutoff—a far piece, in fact—and that'll suit me fine. I'm not anxious to swing for shooting that cowhand."

"You had no choice. He would have killed you—"

"Law in Dodge would be a mite hard to convince that it was self-defense when the reason for it came out. I've got a hunch that rancher, Madden, wears plenty big boots around these parts. His word would carry a lot of weight, and us being pure strangers—"

"Can see what you mean," Hale murmured.

The hoofbeats of the passing posse had died out. Hale took up the reins, shook them to arouse the dozing horses, and glanced at Riley for instructions.

"Cut hard right," Tabor directed. "Take it slow."

"Why? They're gone?" Hale asked, a trace of impatience in his tone.

"Maybe. That marshal just might be smart enough to leave some of his deputies along the road if he figured we'd pulled off somewhere."

"Never thought of that."

"When we get to the edge of the grove, pull up. I'll jump down, go on ahead and have a look around. If there's nobody in sight, I'll give you a signal."

Hale smiled. "I'm beginning to believe running into you was a stroke of good luck—and maybe I ought to take you on as a partner since you know the country and people around here so well. You've got the knack for looking ahead and figuring out the best thing to do."

"Just aiming to keep my neck out of a noose," Riley said. "End of the grove's not far."

They came to the last of the trees a few moments later, and as Adam Hale drew the team to a halt, Riley left the seat. Crouching low, he made his way through the shadows to the shoulder of the road, and hunched there he studied the dusty trace in both directions for as far as he could see, listening intently all the while. He could neither detect nor hear anyone—even the dog at Cimarron had finally ceased its barking. It would be safe to cross, and returning to where the wagon had stopped he beckoned to Hale.

"Clear as it'll ever be," he said, "but drive slow. Can't afford to make any more noise than we have to. Chains jingling and pans rattling just might be heard by somebody back up at the forks on a quiet night like this. I'll walk ahead till we come to the river."

"This crossing—is it a dangerous one?" Hale asked, keeping his voice low.

"Hard to tell how it'll be. I've seen the water high and I've seen it low. If they haven't had a lot of rain upstream it'll be low and we won't have any trouble."

They moved on, the big bay geldings drawing the wagon easily through the loose sand. Shortly they crossed the road and dropped off into the swale that ran down to the Arkan-

sas. Halting at the edge of the river, Riley raised his hand
and Hale again drew the rig to a halt.

"Looks like there's been a washout, but wagons have
been crossing. Plenty of tracks. Expect it'll be safe for us."

Climbing back up onto the seat of the rig, Tabor glanced
at Hale. In the open, bright moonlight shone on his broad,
square-jawed face, revealing the tension that gripped him.
He was probably reliving the minutes when his partner was
lost at such a river crossing back in Ohio, Riley guessed.

"Want me to take the lines?"

Hale shook his head, and flicking the leathers lightly
against the backs of the geldings he began the crossing.

They had no problem, as Riley had anticipated, and in
only a few minutes the powerful span of bays had drawn the
wagon through the hub-deep water and were once more on
solid ground.

Hale, a tight smile now on his face, turned to Riley. "We
go left here, I expect—"

Tabor nodded, his eyes on a distant spot of red well up
the trail. "Somebody ahead of us. Wagon camp. Can see a
fire."

"Could be Indians—"

"Could be, but they won't be hostile. Haven't given folks
any trouble on the trail for quite a spell."

"Glad to hear that," Hale said, relieved. "And a wagon
train would be most welcome. I could use a bit of female
company."

Tabor scrubbed at his jaw. "Like I said before—you best
go careful-like around women out here. Their menfolk don't
take kindly to trifling."

Hale laughed. "Trifling—I like that word, but don't let it
trouble you. I'll use care." He paused, put his direct attention on Riley. "You ought to look at it the same way as I do

—the only real pleasure a man can find in this life is with a woman. That's a fact that even William Shakespeare acknowledged, about three centuries ago."

Riley shrugged. Shakespeare, he vaguely recalled, was someone who wrote poetry, or maybe it was plays, and to him nothing more than a name; but evidently both Hale and Shakespeare had the same idea about women.

"Obliged," he said, "but I expect I'd best stick to the way I was brought up."

"Your choice," Hale said as the wagon rolled steadily along on the well-traveled road. "I can see we have a difference of opinion where women are concerned, but that doesn't make our friendship any less. Agree?"

"Sure," Riley replied, his eyes fixed on the red spot glowing in the distance. He almost hoped that it would be Indians, and not a wagon train, camped along the trail.

4

The fire proved to be that of three wagons camped along the Arkansas. The men came forward, rifles hung in the crooks of their arms, in wary greeting when Hale drew to a halt, but he cheerily ignored their caution, and handing the reins to Riley jumped down from the wagon.

"Name's Adam Hale," he announced jovially, walking up to them with extended arm. "My partner there is Riley Tabor. Your fire was a mighty welcome shine in the night, but no more welcome than seeing you gentlemen."

The attitude of the pilgrims changed, their wariness fading in the face of Hale's charm. One by one they stepped forward and shook his hand.

"If it's all right with you folks, my partner and me will set up camp here—then we can go on together since we're all headed in the same direction. Traveling alone gets mighty lonely."

"You're plenty welcome to throw in with us," one of the pilgrims said. "Just pull your rig close to mine," he added, pointing at the end vehicle in the half circle of wagons.

"We're obliged to you, Mr. Alder," Hale said, and taking the headstall of the near bay in hand, led the rig to the indicated location.

"You'll find plenty of burning wood down along the river," Alder, a tall, mountaineerish-looking man in heavy shoes, sweat-stained undershirt, overalls and a ragged-brimmed black hat, said. "There anything else you might be needing, just holler."

The remainder of the pilgrims had drifted back to their wagons, and as Hale brought the bays to a stop, Alder's family—wife, two small children and a boy in his teens—moved into view from the shadows where they had been standing.

At once Hale strode up to them, and went through the ritual of introduction. Riley, climbing down from his seat on the wagon, heaved a sigh of relief as he began to unhitch the team. Hale would find no womanly attraction where the Alders were concerned. Even in the pale moonlight and the glow of the large fire, built in the center of the half circle, Alder's wife appeared worn and lifeless.

When the bay geldings were free of their harness Riley led them down to the river, where he watered them sparingly, after which he returned to the wagon, dug out the canvas and leather feed bags he had noted earlier, filled them with grain and affixed them to the horses' heads. That done, he looked about for Adam Hale. He spotted the easterner near the center of the half circle of vehicles being introduced in turn by Alder to the other members of the train and their families.

Riley shrugged. He wished, briefly, that he could be as free and outgoing as Hale, but he never had been, and he reckoned he never would be. Coming about, he returned to the wagon, and feeling the need for food, located the chuck box and dug out the coffeepot and frying pan. Filling the pot from the water keg, he carried it and the spider to a nearby horseshoe of blackened rocks arranged by some previous pilgrims for cooking purposes.

Setting the utensils aside, Riley scouted about until he had gathered what he considered enough wood for the night, started a fire and placed the coffeepot over the flames. Going back to the wagon then for the box that contained Hale's supply of grub, he found Adam Hale already carrying it toward him.

"What'll it be?" Hale asked, smiling broadly. "We have canned corn, beans, meat, biscuits—just about anything, in fact, that you've got a feeling for."

Setting the hinged box down near the fire he lay back the lid and exposed the stock of canned goods and preserved food he'd brought along.

"You do the picking," Riley said, taking up the jar of already ground coffee beans and turning to the pot of water beginning to simmer. Adam Hale had come well provided with select, already prepared food which was a handy if expensive convenience.

"Let's make it corn with bacon for our main dish," Hale said, crouching beside the box. "Along with toasted light bread. And we can have preserved peaches and sweet cakes on the side."

Riley nodded his agreement. It wouldn't be much like the trail grub he was accustomed to eating, but more like a meal in some town restaurant; it would be different, he had to admit. Things would change soon, however. They were now in country where canned goods were not as readily available as they had been in Dodge City and points east. By the time they reached the wagon traders at Bent's Fort or the general store at Trinidad, the grub box would be filled with more conventional food—salt pork, beans, potatoes, onions and the like.

"Some real fine people in that wagon train," Adam said, dumping the corn into the spider and beginning to trim slices from the side of bacon. "They're all going to Colorado —some place called Pueblo. Ever been there?"

Riley shook his head. The night was clear and bright, and it was growing colder. Over along the river something made a splash—a fish, he supposed, or it could have been a beaver or a muskrat.

"No, don't recollect ever being there—"

"Alder tried to talk me into changing my plans and going along with them. Told him I had my heart set on going on west."

Hale had finished slicing and cutting the bacon into smaller strips and had placed the pan over the fire. Taking up a short, round loaf of light bread that was wrapped in oiled paper of some sort, he carved off half a dozen inch-thick pieces and laid them on the rocks that contained the fire.

"Expect it will be a smart idea for us to go along with these folks for a few days," Adam said, settling back on his heels. "Having company will be nice."

Riley set the coffeepot, its dark, savory contents now boiling busily, off to the side, and turned to the grub box for cups, plates and tools with which to eat.

"I figure they'll be moving slow," he said. "One of the wagons is being pulled by oxen. If you're in a big hurry—"

"Won't hurt us to loaf along for a bit. It'll do the horses good," Hale said with an indifferent wave of his hand. "I didn't figure you were in a big rush to get somewhere."

"Not—nothing waiting for me, but I'd sure hate for that posse to catch up with us."

"You think there's a chance of that?"

"Maybe not," Riley admitted. "They probably followed the cutoff down far as Middle Springs, and then gave it up. The marshal would figure we're too far away now in some other direction to ever catch up."

"Fine, fine—we'll make this part of the trip as enjoyable as possible."

Riley agreed, and pouring Hale and himself a cup of steaming coffee, settled back to wait on the mixture in the spider. He doubted Adam Hale would be content for long to travel at the pace the Alder train would be moving. But such was up to the easterner. He was the owner of the rig and thus was the one to make all decisions of that nature. He, Riley realized, was only a passenger.

The train, led alternately by the different wagons and their owners, moved out early the next morning, crawling slowly over the hard-packed wagon tracks that ran along the river. Most of the time Tabor did the driving of the Hale rig, simply assuming the chore as he had the cooking and the care of the horses. Adam Hale chose to walk with those of the train who, weary of the heavily laden, lurching, often hard-tailed vehicles, preferred to march alongside their rigs, finding relief in that simple exercise.

On the second day Tabor noticed Hale had paired off with a tall, dark-haired woman who was a member of the family in the lead wagon. Riley, in the vehicle immediately following, watched them as they walked, hand in hand, Hale in animated conversation, the girl laughing and seemingly enjoying Adam's company very much.

That evening Hale disappeared shortly after dark when the meal was over and did not return to the wagon until well onto midnight. This became a pattern for succeeding days and nights, and then abruptly, while he and Riley were eating breakfast one fine, warm morning, Adam Hale announced they were moving on.

"Train's too slow. Going to take forever to get anywhere

at this pace." He paused, looked squarely at Riley. "That all right with you?"

"Suits me," Tabor replied, and an hour later they had hitched up the bays, loaded the wagon, and were pulling away.

"You already said your good-byes?" Riley asked. He personally had kept pretty much to himself, it not being his nature to be overly friendly.

"Last night," Hale replied.

On the trail again, and out ahead of the other wagons, Riley looked back—a habit he had fallen into since eluding the Dodge City marshal's posse back near Cimarron. There were no riders in sight, but the dark-haired woman with whom Adam had become acquainted was standing a few yards apart from the wagon train watching him and Hale depart. There was a kind of loneliness to her, a melancholia that sobered Riley Tabor and saddened him.

"How far to Bent's Fort?"

"Take a week or so—depending," Riley answered, glancing about at the landmarks. Down on the river several ducks were quacking noisily, and on its far side a solitary horse, a stray apparently, grazed on the short grass.

"Depending on what?"

"On how hard you want to push the team."

"They're in fine condition. So far the trip hasn't hurt them one whit."

"The off horse needs shoeing."

"Can take care of that when we get to this Bent's Fort," Hale said. "I've got a box of shoes and plenty of nails in the back of the wagon. If you can't do it maybe we can find somebody there who can."

"Done my share of shoeing," Riley said. "I can do it if we can find a forge."

"Good. Whip up the team. Let's put some miles behind us before sunset. It's going to be a long, lonesome ride unless we catch up to another wagon train."

5

Late in the afternoon they overtook another train, this one
of only two wagons belonging to one family. Hale, in his
usual cheery fashion, introduced himself and Tabor, easily
making friends with the pilgrims, the Sanduskys.

Kentuckians en route to Utah, or maybe on to Oregon,
the family consisted of the father, Amos—a tall, lanky,
straight-faced man with a pointed beard; Rose, his wife—
small, wiry, and like most mountain women showing the
effects of years of toil; and three sons and a daughter—
Willie, the youngest; Jess, small like his mother; Asa, a du-
plicate of his father; and the daughter, eighteen-year-old
Lucy. She was blonde, blue-eyed, well shaped and with a
bubbly personality, and she instantly captivated Adam
Hale.

"Undoubtedly another Aphrodite!" he declared. "And if
I were Paris I'd certainly award her the prize for womanly
beauty!"

Riley had no idea who Aphrodite was, and he'd always
thought Paris was a city in France, but Hale made it sound
like it was a person. Riley gave it little thought, however;
both names stemmed from Adam's vast store of book learning—but he did agree that Lucy Sandusky was about the
prettiest girl he'd ever laid eyes on.

The Sandusky wagons moved a bit faster than those of
the Alder party, thanks probably to the good condition of

their horses. For the next several days, during which Hale spent much time with Lucy walking alongside the train, or making brief forays off to the side on the trail to investigate some attraction, the journey was quite pleasant.

In the evenings all would gather around the campfire, where talk about the day's activities and problems would take place while steaming cups of chicory were drunk. Eventually Lucy would begin a song, at which point her brothers and occasionally all of the others would join in, and the worrisome tribulations of the day would disappear.

Adam Hale took a big hand in it, so much so that an outsider coming upon the party would think him a member of the Sandusky family. Riley, reticent by nature, was forever on the fringe, and while he greatly enjoyed the campfire gatherings he remained quiet and reserved where the singing and conversation were concerned.

Never a very friendly man, Riley had been a cowhand all his adult life, and at twenty-one years of age he had no particular desire to be anything else. Near six feet in height and weighing a lean hundred and seventy pounds, he had deep-set dark eyes, almost black hair, and conditions permitting was usually clean-shaven. At the moment, sprawled at the edge of the fire's glow, he was wearing the only clothing he had: red shirt, faded tan pants, new boots he'd only recently purchased in Dodge City, leather vest, yellow neckerchief and a brown, wide-brimmed, Texas-style hat.

"You sure you don't want any more of Ma's cobbler?"

At Lucy Sandusky's unexpected question Tabor sat up hurriedly. "No ma'am," he replied. "It's truly good, but I ate all I could handle. Thank you just the same."

"Certainly," Lucy responded with her wide smile, and moved on with the square pan of apple pie to offer it to the others.

"How much farther is it to Bent's Fort?" Riley heard Amos Sandusky say.

"Only a few more days," Hale replied, "but you best ask Tabor. He knows more about it than I . . . Miss Lucy, it's such a lovely evening, why don't we take a stroll along the river?"

The girl handed the pan of cobbler to her mother, picked up a knitted shawl and draped it about her shoulders. Smiling brightly to the easterner, she crossed to where he was standing.

"Better keep an eye out for redskins," Asa Sandusky said jokingly. "Been seeing a few parties camped along the river —and I'll bet they'd sure fancy that yellow hair of yours, little sister."

Lucy tossed her head in gesture of girlish defiance and took a firm grip on Hale's arm. "I'll have plenty of protection," she said. "Anyway, these aren't hostile Indians."

Hale laughed. "Don't worry, she'll be safe with me," he said as they moved off into the moon- and star-lit night.

"That so—it'll still be a few days till we get to the fort?"

The elder Sandusky's voice broke into Riley's thoughts as he watched Hale and the girl fade into the semi-darkness. "He's about right. From here I'd say we're three days out."

"Three days!" Jess Sandusky echoed. "Pa, I ain't sure that wheel will go that far—"

Jess was driving the lighter and smaller of the Sandusky wagons, one not so well adapted for lengthy traveling.

"We'll work on it in the morning, try and fix it so's it'll hold together till we get to that fort. Can maybe scare up a wheelwright or a blacksmith that'll—"

"Seems you've got the wrong idea about Bent's Fort," Riley interrupted. "Hardly anything there now—maybe a trader or two. Fort itself's nothing but ruins."

Rose Sandusky gasped. "Why, we planned to fill our larder there! We're getting low on some things we—"

"You say the fort's closed?" Sandusky cut in, his voice reflecting surprise.

Riley frowned, considering the Kentuckian. "Don't know who you've been talking to but there ain't been nothing at Bent's Fort, other'n wagon traders—and they're not always around—for years."

"You're talking about the old fort," Asa Sandusky said, "the one that burned down in 'fifty, or maybe it was earlier. We're meaning the new one."

"One you call the new one's in the same shape. Hardly anything there—and it's the one I'm talking about."

"Won't there be a place where we can buy grub?" Amos said in a worried voice. "We're needing stuff."

"There'll be a trader there, maybe a couple. They'll have their wagons loaded if they haven't already sold out to folks ahead of us. Prices will be high, but if you're needing something bad, best you pay. Next place we'll come to after we leave the fort where there'll be a general store is a settlement called Trinidad."

Rose Sandusky sighed wearily; one of her sons, Jess, rose, crossed to her side and laid a comforting arm about her thin shoulders.

"Now, don't you worry none, Ma, we'll make out."

"Sure, we'll get by. Always have," Amos said, reassuringly, and rising glanced off toward the river. "About time that girl was getting back."

"She ain't been gone long, Pa," Asa said, throwing more wood on the fire. "Expect she'll be showing up soon."

Riley Tabor drew himself to his feet, and nodding to the Sanduskys started for the Hale wagon. Lucy and Adam Hale would return, he had little doubt of that, but it would be in Adam's own good time—just as it had been for the last two nights.

Each time Hale and the girl had gone for a stroll—absences that usually lasted for an hour or longer—Amos Sandusky had shown a growing impatience that bordered on suspicion. Hale was treading on thin ice, that was certain, and later that night, when Hale rejoined him at the wagon, Riley felt it wise to warn him.

"None of my put-in, but you best have a care where that girl, Lucy, is concerned. Her pa is starting to wonder about those long walks you take."

Hale laughed as he pulled off his boots. "Let him wonder. No harm in the girl going for a stroll with me."

"I reckon not," Tabor drawled, "long as that's all there is to it."

"You any reason to think otherwise?" Hale demanded, an edge to his voice.

"Nope," Riley answered, "other than the way I know you think about women—what they're for."

"All of which comes under the heading of my business, not yours," Hale snapped. "You hold your peace, Tabor. Just do the driving and other chores. That's all I expect of you."

Riley shrugged. "Figure I'm doing you a favor, warning you."

It was an open break insofar as he was concerned, and he couldn't get to New Mexico, or some other familiar area where he could leave Hale, any too soon. Meanwhile he had no choice but to continue as a passenger on the easterner's wagon, paying his fare by handling the team and sharing the various other tasks.

That Adam Hale lent no weight to the cautioning words Riley had spoken was evident the next evening as well as those that followed. Each night at campfire he and Lucy Sandusky would pair off and disappear into the night for an hour or so. And during the day they were often together as well.

Riley said no more to Hale, feeling that he had done his part to warn the man of the possible consequences he was courting; he felt that now it was up to Hale.

The days dragged on with the train being compelled to move slower than at first because of the weak wheel on one of the Sandusky vehicles, but around midmorning of a bright, sunny day an irregular tan and gray formation appeared on the western horizon.

"That Bent's Fort?" Hale asked from his place on the seat beside Tabor.

Riley nodded. "That's it—or what's left of it. Ought to get there this afternoon, early."

Hale said nothing, but twisting about he jumped to the ground, hurried ahead to the smaller of the Sandusky wagons in which Lucy was riding and drew himself aboard. Shortly both Adam and the girl climbed down, and as they had done many times, began to walk beside the wagon—and eventually strayed off into the bushy growth along the shoulders of the road.

6

There were two traders at the ruins of the fort, one a squat, bustling merchant who introduced himself as Sol Steinberg, the other a ruddy, smiling German who said his name was Hans Bruemmer. They had parked their wagons, well loaded with foodstuff, clothing, woolen blankets and other trail necessities, a hundred feet apart in the area that lay between the Arkansas River and the crumbling remains of the fort. As the train drew close, each of the merchants began hawking his wares.

"There anything we need?" Hale asked as Riley drew the wagon to a stop. Ahead of them both Sandusky vehicles had pulled up to Bruemmer's, and already Rose Sandusky was hurriedly dismounting as if anxious to be first in line and thus have the pick of the traveling merchant's stock. There was no need for haste—no other pilgrims were in sight, although several black scars of campfires indicated the recent passage of other pilgrims.

"Can use some coffee and lard, and a sack of flour," Riley said, his attention now on a bearded old man coming slowly toward them from the ruins. Dressed in stained, fringed buckskins, a round leather hat and moccasins, he carried a long-barreled rifle in the crook of his arm. There was something familiar to the look of the oldster that held Tabor's eyes.

"Here's a double eagle," Riley heard Hale say, and

turned as the man pressed the gold coin into his hand. "You buy whatever we need. If that's not enough money, pay it out of your own pocket and I'll square up with you later."

"You going somewhere?"

Hale smiled and nodded. "Little personal business," he replied and dropping to the ground moved off toward the Sandusky wagons. "I think little Miss Lucy and I will explore what's left of the fort."

Riley shook his head in disapproval, wrapped the lines about the whipstock and climbed down from the seat. Steinberg hurried forward, a smile on his face.

"Whatever you need I've got it—at a reasonable price! Groceries, bedding, clothing, horseshoes—"

"Sack of flour, salt, coffee, a tin of lard," Riley began, and as the merchant drew forth a dog-eared notepad and a pencil, named off a few other articles that he remembered were in short supply.

Over at the Bruemmer wagon the entire Sandusky clan had gathered about the German's vehicle, its sides now raised and propped open so that customers might better see the merchandise. Lucy appeared to have small interest in the bargaining. She was standing a bit to the rear, her eyes on Adam Hale who was hurrying toward her.

"Hey there, friend, ain't you that Tabor fellow?"

At the sound of his name Riley came about. It was the yellow-bearded old man he'd seen coming from the fort. A smile cracked his mouth.

"Jack—Kansas Jack!" he said, and extended his hand. "Might've known I'd find you still hanging around here."

Kansas Jack brushed his hat to the back of his head. "Now, where the hell else would I be? Was here when Bill built the place, and was right here when he shut her down."

Kansas Jack—Riley had never known the old scout, trapper and buffalo hunter by any other name—kept himself in grub and other necessities by occasionally serving as a guide for hunting parties, or for pilgrims taking a route different from the established trail.

"And I reckon you'll still be here when you cash in your chips," Riley said. "You got any of that rotgut you call whiskey over at your camp?"

"Nary a drop," Jack replied. "Things ain't been so good around here lately—but I expect old Sol's got a jug or two he'd part with for hard money."

Steinberg, busy assembling the items ordered by Tabor from his stock, paused, glanced around. "You say something about whiskey?"

"Sure did—whiskey," Jack answered. "We'll just have us a jug—and we ain't figuring to pay you no fancy price, neither!"

"I ain't ever crooked you, Jack," Steinberg said in an injured tone. "Not right you should say that I—"

"All right—I didn't mean it!" the old trapper said, reaching for the jug the merchant handed him. "How much'll it be?"

"Dollar and a half. I carted it all the way from—"

"Dollar and a half!" Kansas Jack shouted so loud that a dozen or so prairie dogs watching from the safety of their village a fair distance away hastily ducked into their holes. "That there's plain robbery, Sol—and you dang sure know it!"

"Make it a dollar then," Steinberg said wearily. "I wish to hell you'd stay away from here when I'm doing business."

Kansas Jack nodded, satisfied. "Now that's some better. Why, I recollect the day when a man could buy himself a barrel of Taos Lightning for five dollars!"

"That was way back when there was buffalo running everywhere," Steinberg observed acidly. "You're still living in the past. About time you woke up . . . Your order's ready, mister. You sure you don't need no blankets—or maybe a real heavy coat? You'll be needing something warm if you're heading up into Colorado Territory."

"No, got everything else I need—we're going south. How much do I owe you—including the whiskey?"

Steinberg bobbed, consulted his pad of paper. "For a good customer like you that did no whining and complaining I'll throw in the whiskey. Bill comes up to a little over thirty dollars. I'll make it an even thirty."

The prices traders charged for their goods was always a shock to Riley Tabor, but he long ago had realized there was nothing to do but pay. Digging into his pocket for the double eagle Hale had given him and obtaining the balance from his money belt, he squared up with the trader and then turned to Kansas Jack.

"Help me load this grub into the wagon, then you and me can set down in the shade and do some serious drinking. Like to know if anybody I know've come through this year."

Taking up an armload of the articles purchased, Tabor started for the wagon. Only Mrs. Sandusky was to be seen now at Bruemmer's, the men being inside the vehicles rearranging their loads, or off elsewhere for some reason. There was no sign of Lucy and Adam Hale. Likely they were still probing about in the ruins of the old fort.

Depositing as much of the food in the grub box as it would hold, Riley stowed the remainder in the chest used for pots and pans, and leaving the wagon returned to where Kansas Jack, having done his part, was squatting on his heels, waiting. Steinberg again voiced his thanks, reminding

Tabor as he did that if there was anything else needed he would still be around.

"Reckon we as well set right here in the shade of your rig," the old trapper said, and leaning back against a wheel drew the cork from the jug with his strong teeth. "Sure is a mighty fine outfit you've got."

"Not mine," Riley said, taking a place beside the old man. "Just riding in it—sort of working my way back to home."

"Thought I seen another fellow up there on the seat with you," Jack said, taking another swig from the jug. "Real high-toned-looking fellow. What happened to him?"

"Said he was going to have a look at what's left of the fort," Riley answered, and had his drink of the fiery liquor.

"Sure ain't much left," Jack said, letting his watery old eyes drift over the remains of the buildings. "A mighty shame, too. Was twice as fine a place as the first one William and Charlie built up near the Picketwire, but it sure weren't as comforting, can tell you that. Ain't nothing like the feeling it gives a man when he come out of the hills after tramping through snow up to his hind end all day, and looked down on the place—fires a'going, smoke hanging in the air, and folks moving about inside the walls. Yes sir, them Bents done this part of the country a fine thing when they built the old fort."

A man named Cerain St. Vrain had much to do with building it, too, Riley recalled, and then remembered that Kansas Jack had no use for St. Vrain for some reason and would never mention his name.

"I recollect you never did see the old fort when it was going good," Jack said, taking another pull at the jug. "Why, the wall they built around the place to keep out the hostiles was fifteen, maybe twenty feet high. There was places for lookouts at each end, and the courtyard, as William called it, was a good two hundred feet long, maybe half that wide."

"I remember you telling me about it," Tabor said, trying to break in on the old trapper's endless narration. He was hoping to get some news about the ranchers on to the west before he set to work on the loose shoe of the off horse. "Any of the Box K cowhands been by lately?"

"Was all kinds of stuff a man could trade his peltries for," Kansas Jack droned on. "And there was always plenty of smoking tobacco, and whiskey and young squaws for a man to dance with. Now, I recollect—"

Riley drew himself slowly erect. Coming at a run from the upper end of the ruins was Lucy. She was heading for the Sandusky wagons and her mother who had moved out to meet her. Evidently something had happened—an accident perhaps, Tabor thought. Hale could have fallen. At that moment the girl saw him, and slowed.

"Pa—my brothers—they've got Adam!" she cried, and hurried on toward the older woman.

Riley swore deeply. Hale had got himself in trouble again over a woman—deep trouble if he was any judge of the Sanduskys—and bailing out the man a second time, especially after he'd been warned, didn't set well. But Tabor guessed he owed it to Hale to step in and help him out of the jam he was in.

"Come on, Jack," he said, turning to the old trapper. "Could be I'll be needing your help."

"Doing what?" Kansas Jack asked, struggling to his feet, rifle in one hand, finger of the other hooked in the whiskey jug's handle.

"Got a hunch that friend of mine's got himself in a bad picklement," Riley answered as he climbed up onto the seat of the wagon and extended a hand to aid the older man. "Hang on!" he added, and gathering up the reins wheeled the wagon about and started across the open ground for the fort.

They reached the crumbling remains of the forward wall, the wagon rocking and jolting wildly as the horses raced over the uneven ground. Legs braced, hanging tight to the lines, Riley swept the interior of the old fort with his eyes for some sign of Hale and the Sanduskys.

Motion far over to his left caught his attention. It was in an area partly blocked off by the remains of a stone wall. Instantly Tabor veered the team toward it, cutting it so sharply that the wagon tipped dangerously onto two wheels for several moments.

"Goddammit!" Kansas Jack yelled in alarm as he gripped the handrail of the seat. "You a'trying to kill us?"

Riley made no reply. They had reached a point where he could see beyond the old wall. A mixture of anger and exasperation shook Tabor. Adam Hale had gone too far again. The Sanduskys had him tied to a post, apparently once a part of a porch, and the elder member of the family was lashing his bare back with a leather belt. Bloody stripes marked the places where the blows were landing, but during it all Hale, head forward and resting against the post, was uttering no sound.

"He's had enough!" Riley shouted, bringing the team to a halt, and drawing his gun.

Amos Sandusky, face grim and glistening with sweat, paused and turned.

"This—this no-account," he said in a trembling voice, "has gone and disgraced my family and my daughter. We caught him in the act. I aim to make him pay with his blood."

"Cut him loose," Tabor said sternly, and motioning to Kansas Jack climbed down from the seat. "You've whipped him plenty. Now leave him be."

"No, I ain't done with him yet—"

Riley drew his weapon and fired a shot at the feet of the older man. "Yes, you are," he snapped, and then, shifting the gun to cover the three boys who were standing off to one side, repeated: "Cut him loose."

Jess Sandusky shrugged, and drawing his knife stepped up to the post and slashed the rawhide cord that tied Hale's wrists together. The man sagged as he was released but caught himself.

"He's sure a sore mess," Riley heard Kansas Jack mutter as they dismounted. "Ain't no man deserving of a beating like that."

Riley was inclined to disagree but he made no comment. Hale moved slowly and painfully away from the post. Crossing to where his shirt and hat lay, he picked them up and started for the wagon. Riley, gun in hand, took him by the arm, but Adam jerked angrily away and continued walking in stiff, measured steps toward the wagon.

Hale had covered half the distance when Amos Sandusky lunged forward as if to prevent the man's leaving. Immediately Kansas Jack brought up his rifle and leveled it menacingly at him and the others.

"Now, just you stay put there, friend," he warned. "Mean that for all of you fellows. You just don't do nothing till Tabor and his friend are aboard that wagon—and are gone."

Adam Hale had reached the vehicle, and still refusing any help climbed up onto the seat. Tossing the clothing into the wagonbed, he put his hands together in his lap and, head down, slumped forward. Tabor, wasting no time, quickly took his place beside him.

"I ain't done with you yet!" Amos Sandusky yelled, shaking his fist. "I aim to see you dead if it's the last thing I ever do!"

Hale stirred, raised his head and faced the older man. "No, I should kill you," he said in a low, savage tone. "You whipped me like I was a dog. I ought to pick up this rifle laying at my feet and blow your head off—but for your daughter's sake I won't."

"You better do your shooting right now," Sandusky said, "because me and the boys'll be hunting you down, and you just maybe won't ever get your chance again to—"

"Well, you ain't doing nothing right now but standing real quiet," Kansas Jack cut in. Twisting his head slightly he nodded to Riley. "Move out. I'll keep these jaspers a'cooling their heels till you're a far piece down the way."

Riley took up the lines and put the team into motion. "You handle them all right?"

"Sure, sure. I don't reckon none of them wants a taste of old Betsy's lead . . . So long, and take care."

"So long," Tabor replied as he kicked off the brake and swung the wagon sharply about. "I'm obliged to you."

"This here's what friends are for, ain't it?" he heard Jack reply as the wagon, bouncing and rattling over the broken ground, headed for the road.

7

Reaching the opening in the fort's crumbling wall, Riley swerved the team toward the road. Off to his left he could see Lucy Sandusky and her mother, arms about each other, watching him race by. Farther down, both Bruemmer and Sol Steinberg had walked a short distance from their wagons—their attention, curious and wondering, also on him.

"God—slow down—too rough," Hale groaned as the left front wheel of the vehicle struck a rock that sent them bounding high into the air and then back to solid ground with a bone-jarring jolt. "Can't stand—"

"You'll have to," Riley snapped. "Got to get the hell out of here fast! Jack won't be able to hold that bunch for long."

As the rig straightened out on the well-defined trail, Tabor threw a glance back over his shoulder. Asa and Jess Sandusky were just leaving the compound of the fort, and were running hard toward their wagons. They had somehow managed to get away from Kansas Jack, either overpowering or slipping away from him. Since there were just the two of them it was likely Jack still had the other Sanduskys under control.

Asa and Jess wouldn't try to follow in one of the family vehicles, that was certain. They would unhitch two of the horses and attempt to overtake Hale and Tabor on them. It would take several minutes to strip the harness from the team, and the horses, accustomed to pulling a wagon rather than being ridden, would be slow to respond.

"My back—got to do something about it," Hale said, raising his voice to be heard above the horses, now at full gallop.

Riley again glanced back. The Sanduskys had not gotten under way as yet, but now the other brother, Willie, and their father, Amos, had rejoined them. On beyond them Kansas Jack, the long gun he affectionately called Old Betsy on his shoulder, was making his way slowly out of the fort's compound toward Sol Steinberg's wagon.

"There's a turnoff ahead a couple of miles that leads down to the river," Tabor said, turning to Hale. "I'll take it. Can pull up in the trees out of sight and do some doctoring. Just have to hope the Sanduskys don't spot us."

"They chasing us?"

"What they've got in mind," Riley said, taking up the whip and cracking it over the backs of the bays. "Last time I looked they hadn't mounted up yet."

Adam reached back to the clothing he had thrown behind the seat and selected his outer shirt. Gingerly draping it over his shoulders, he shook his head.

"Never thought matters with that girl would turn out this way."

Riley, keeping the team at a dead gallop while glancing back over the trail from time to time, shrugged. "Best you remember how men feel about their womenfolks out here."

"I know, I know," Hale said wearily. "You've told me, but it's no different where I come from." He stiffened suddenly as a rough place in the road brought the shirt in contact with the raw wounds on his back. "When we get to this place along the river you're talking about, you'll find a medicine box in the wagonbed somewhere. There's a jar of

salve in it. Supposed to be for burns but I expect it'll do as
well for those welts on my back."

Riley Tabor shook his head as the team raced on, the
wagon sometimes rolling smoothly over a grassy area, other
times bouncing and whipping back and forth when it
crossed a rocky, uneven stretch of the trail.

"Swallow of the whiskey in that jug there might help you
some," Riley suggested during a particularly bad moment
that left the wounded man groaning.

Hale took up the jug, had a deep swallow. Immediately
he set the container aside and spat out what he had in his
mouth.

"Damn stuff tastes like creosote mixed with coal oil!" he
said.

"Probably what it is," Riley replied with a smile. "But
it'll help kill the pain when I start dressing those cuts. Better load up now, we're about to the turnoff."

"You think it's safe to stop? The Sanduskys—"

"No sign of them. Maybe we outran them—at least for a
spell." Riley paused. "You were lucky. That old man was
out to kill you."

"Damn near did," Hale said, and despite his distaste for
the mountain liquor took another swallow from the jug.

Maybe Adam Hale had learned something from the incident. Riley hoped so. It just could be that the next time he'd
not be able to bail Adam out of the trouble he insisted on
getting himself into.

But history began to repeat itself, insofar as Adam Hale
and his womanly conquests were concerned, only days later
as they were entering the treacherous Raton Pass area.

Hale had weathered the treatment of his lacerated back
well, and now, recovered, had resumed their system of trad-

ing off the driving chore with Tabor. They had seen no more of the Sanduskys, although Riley had heard horses on the road not long after he had driven the wagon down into the dense growth along the river that first day. Likely it had been Asa and Jess, but he hadn't bothered to see—he'd been too busy cleaning Hale's punished back and shoulders, and applying the ointment he'd found in the medicine chest.

Riley had purposely avoided Fort Lyon and spent but little time in Trinidad, where it had been necessary to buy grain for the horses and have the shoe on the off bay secured. In the back of Tabor's mind was the possibility that a determined marshal in Dodge City could have put out word to other lawmen requesting the arrest of him and Adam Hale, and he wanted to take no chances. Once in New Mexico, Riley felt such danger would diminish and he could forget using such care. Too, there were the Sanduskys; he recalled the family planned to swing right at the forks that led northward into Colorado and the settlement of Pueblo, but he was not banking on their doing so. Vengeance-minded, Amos and his sons just might continue to search for Adam Hale.

With the easterner handling the lines they had caught up with a family named McKenzie just above the tollhouse at the foot of Raton Pass. The rancher with his wife, Patience, and daughter Annalee were coming down from Colorado, where they had been visiting relatives. McKenzie had a large, well-equipped wagon drawn by four strong horses. There were others at the Wooten stone house also—pilgrims, teamsters, soldiers, Indians—but it wasn't in them that Hale immediately became interested; it was in the McKenzie family—most particularly Annalee.

John McKenzie—in his early fifties, like his heavy-set, sunbonneted wife—was the typical rancher. Weathered, narrow-eyed and hard-jawed, he had wrested a good life for himself and his family as a cattle grower from the raw and untamed region of northeastern New Mexico Territory, and it was apparent from the deference accorded him by Dick Wooten and others at the tollhouse that he was well thought of and highly respected.

Hale had ingratiated himself at once with the McKenzies, drawing the man aside often and asking him countless questions about the territory, ranching, cattle, the market and other pertinent information. Tabor, readying the rig for the hard, five-day pull over the pass, was not fully convinced that Adam was all that interested in growing beef, and it seemed to him that Hale always managed somehow to hold his conversations with the rancher when Annalee—about twenty, with wide-set brown eyes, honey-colored hair, and a shapely body—was present nearby.

But he remembered Hale had declared he was coming into the West to make investments, and it could be he was simply seeking to learn from the experiences of McKenzie and asking for advice. At any rate Riley reckoned he should give Adam the benefit of the doubt and assume the man was sincere in making his inquiries and was not simply getting himself better acquainted with the girl.

On the second day, however, as the string of seven wagons slowly ascended the steep, winding trail, Tabor knew he was wrong. Hale, handling the lines at the time, handed them over to Riley, and turned to leap down from the wagon.

"Don't feel much like driving," he said. "Think I'll see if young Miss McKenzie would like to do a bit of walking with me." He paused, looking out over the towering, mountainous country, brown now in the summer sun. "You ever see a prettier woman than that Annalee?"

"No, can't say as I have," Riley replied in a heavy voice.

Hale was back to his old ways—out to make Annalee McKenzie another of his conquests. Tabor swore quietly. He'd had enough. When they reached Willow Springs, the settlement at the foot of the pass, he'd tell Hale he was through, that he was leaving him.

"Way I feel about her, too," Hale said, going to the ground. "I'll repeat your remark to her. It will make a good opening for me."

Riley watched Adam move ahead, his tall, square-shouldered shape erect and impressive. Time and wear had begun to have their way with the corduroy suit, but Riley had to admit Hale still cut a fine figure of a man.

That was the beginning of Hale's daily strolls alongside the wagons with Annalee McKenzie, just as it had been with Lucy Sandusky, and before her the dark-haired woman with the Alder wagon train—only there was a difference. He and the girl were never out of sight of the others—due to the nature of the pass—and at night all were required to stay close to their vehicles. There had been trouble with renegade Arapaho Indians, and it was deemed unsafe for anyone to leave camp.

Riley noticed the effect the restrictions had on Hale, and as the days and nights dragged slowly by it was apparent the man was growing dissatisfied with his failure to be alone with Annalee McKenzie. Tabor, fully aware that it was none of his business, still felt compelled to comment on it.

"How are things going with you and the McKenzie girl?"

Hale swore impatiently. "I can't get anywhere with her— no matter what I say or do!"

Riley, secretly pleased, clucked softly. "Too bad. She's a real beauty."

"And she knows it!" Hale said, pausing to note a wagon

that pulled off to the side of the trail. One of the leather traces had broken and two men were working feverishly to repair it before they fell too far behind the train.

"She's after a Faustian bargain—and I'm not ready for that."

Tabor frowned, rubbed at his jaw. "What the hell's a Faustian bargain?"

Hale did not laugh at the irritation in Tabor's tone. "A trade I expect you'd call it. If she, well, if she spends some time with me enjoying the good things of life then I'm to marry her when we reach her father's ranch."

Riley shrugged. "Not such a bad trade—"

"Is for me! I'm not ready to marry any woman, not even one as beauteous and desirable as she."

"Then I reckon you'll just have to forget adding her scalp to your belt."

"I'm not finished trying yet!" Hale declared, pulling off his hat and running long fingers through his thick, dark hair. "Heard one of the teamsters tell McKenzie that we'd camp tonight in a good place—one where there'd be plenty of grass and trees and no Indian scare. I just might get my way with Miss Annalee McKenzie there."

But if Adam Hale succeeded his success was not reflected by his demeanor that next morning. Silent, morose, he sat beside Riley on the seat for most of the early hours of that fifth day keeping utterly to himself. When the pilgrims halted at noon to rest the teams and have a bit of lunch, he walked over to the McKenzie wagon, where he soon paired off with Annalee. Riley saw no more of them after that, as one of the men in the wagon behind called on him for help in doing a bit of repair work on their vehicle.

When he returned to the wagon Riley found Hale already

on the seat. Adam had a plate in his lap on which were two thick beef sandwiches.

"Compliments of Mrs. McKenzie," he explained as Tabor climbed aboard and took his place. "Said she thought we just might appreciate some good food."

"The lady's right," Riley replied as Hale took up the lines and, kicking off the brake, put the team into motion. "I'm going to enjoy mine."

As if anxious to finish the arduous journey through the pass as soon as possible, three of the pilgrims were already on the trail and moving. Holding back to allow John McKenzie to fall in ahead of them, in the rancher's customary place, Hale waited, and when there was sufficient clearance swung the bays into the line. The three remaining vehicles then took their customary spots behind, and the train strung out to resume the accomplishment of the pass.

Hale, finished with his sandwich, fell silent. Hunched forward on the seat, elbows on his knees, reins slack, and features stolid, he allowed the team to maintain a pace in accordance with the rest of the wagon. And then abruptly, as they topped out a rise and began a gentle descent, Adam suddenly came to life.

"The hell with this!" he declared angrily. "I'm sick of this creeping along. I'm going on ahead!"

Shouting at the team, he jerked the whip from its holder, cracked it over the horses' heads, and sharply cutting left, swerved out of the line and started down the grade at an increasing speed.

Startled, Riley threw his unfinished sandwich aside, braced his feet solidly against the floor of the quickly swaying wagon, and took a firm grip of the metal arm of the seat. Men were yelling at them as they raced past other wagons, some in protest, others in warning.

"Better slow down," Riley shouted above the clatter of the vehicle and the pound of the bays' hooves. "Some bad turns ahead."

Hale's features were set. "Don't worry about it—I can handle my team—"

"What's the big hurry?"

"Already told you—plain tired of the slow going. Besides, this town at the foot of the pass—Willow Springs—I aim to get there soon as I can, find myself a saloon and get roaring drunk or—"

"Look out!" Tabor shouted in alarm as they careened around a curve. "Best you give me the lines!"

"No—I can handle it," Hale shouted back.

The wagon went up on two wheels, those suddenly in the air spinning madly. It slammed back down, slewed broadside, straightened out briefly, and again began to tip as dust boiled about them.

"Jump!" Riley yelled. "We're going over!"

8

Riley Tabor returned to consciousness slowly. He first became aware of thumping and clattering going on somewhere
close by, and of the brilliant blue sky high overhead. And
then there was movement beside him, and straining to focus
his blurred vision he recognized Annalee and Patience Mc-
Kenzie.

He started to rise, the remembrance of the preceding few
minutes—Adam Hale's taut features, the wildly running
team, the wagon swaying drunkenly as it raced down the
grade—all flooding into his clearing mind.

"No—stay quiet," the older woman said, gently pressing
him back. "You're not hurt, at least we don't think so."
Turning her head, she called: "John! He's come to."

McKenzie, followed by a dozen other members of the
wagon train, came up at a brisk walk. The rancher hunched
down next to his wife and placed a hand on Tabor's shoulder.

"Mighty glad to see you're back with us. You hurting
any?"

"Some. Nothing to complain about."

"You were lucky. You jumped and got clear of the wagon.
Partner of yours wasn't able to."

Riley sat up slowly, unrestrained this time by anyone.
Frowning, he glanced about at Annalee, the rancher, Patience.

"You saying Hale's dead?"

McKenzie nodded. "Got caught under the wagon when it went over."

Shocked, Tabor said nothing. McKenzie handed him a bandanna in which were several gold and silver coins, a roll of currency and a pearl-handled jackknife. Riley stared at the articles woodenly.

"Here's what was on him," the rancher said. "We rocked the wagon back up on its wheels. Don't seem to be any big damage other'n to one of the top bows. Could be one of the wheels got loosened up a bit."

"Horses come out of it pretty good, too," a man standing behind McKenzie said. "The off horse fell, got hisself tangled up in the harness, but we got things straightened out and put him back on his feet. Skinned his front leg a mite but I doctored him with some liniment I had."

"Obliged to you—obliged to all of you," Riley said dully, thrusting the bandanna and its contents into a pocket; then, aided by McKenzie, he drew himself upright.

For several moments his senses swam, and as pain shot through him the realization came that he had evidently hit his head on something other than the ground when he leaped from the careening wagon. Raising his arm he carefully probed the area back of an ear with his fingers. There was a wetness. Blood.

"You are hurt!" Annalee said. "I'm taking you over to our wagon and fixing up that cut!"

"Not all that bad," Tabor said, wiping the tips of his fingers on his bandanna, and accepting his hat from one of the pilgrims who had retrieved it from the rocks along the side of the road. "Don't bother."

"Better go on, let her fix you up," John McKenzie advised. "She's stubborn—and she always gets her way."

Riley smiled. He'd heard about Annalee's willfulness from Hale. Likely, if she had given in to him and not insisted on her way, Adam would be alive at that moment. But there was no point in thinking about it. What was done was done, and nothing anyone could do would bring Hale back to the land of the living.

"What do you want us to do with the dead man?" one of the pilgrims asked. "You wanting us to go ahead and bury him along the trail like we usually do, or you wanting something else?"

Riley glanced at McKenzie for a suggestion. "Whatever's right. I don't know where he's from or who his kin is—or even if he has any."

The rancher scrubbed at his jaw thoughtfully. "Was no papers on him, only that money and knife. All you know about him is his name?"

"That's all, and the fact that he came from Pennsylvania. Never did say what town."

McKenzie shrugged. "Guess the only thing to do is bury him right here. You go along with Annalee. I'll see to him being taken care of properly."

Riley and the girl made their way to the McKenzie wagon. Patience was there ahead of them, moving about inside the covered vehicle as she located and finally brought out the small satchel that was the medicine kit. Pointing to a stool that she had also produced, she nodded to Riley.

"Sit there," she directed, and as Tabor settled onto the piece of crude furniture, added: "Take his hat, Annalee."

"I'll look after him, Mama," the girl said coolly, and handing Tabor's hat to the older woman she took possession of the medicine kit.

Patience McKenzie shrugged indifferently; then, laying Riley's hat in the back of the wagon, she moved off to where several other women had gathered. Up near the Hale wagon the thud of picks and spades breaking the sun-baked earth could be heard as the men of the train prepared a grave for Adam Hale.

"This is going to sting," Annalee warned. "It's really not much of a cut but it could get infected and mortify."

"Still don't figure it's worth bothering with," Tabor said, flinching when the medicine Annalee applied came in contact with raw flesh. "Been hurt worse falling off a horse."

Annalee made no comment, and then after a moment or two: "Did Adam tell you about me?"

The girl's question caught Riley by surprise. He gave it thought, nodded. "Yeh, reckon he did. Was plenty taken by you."

"He mentioned that you had paid me a nice compliment," Annalee said. "I want to thank you . . . Now, where's that salve. I need to apply some."

"Was only speaking the truth—"

"There, that should take care of it," Annalee said, when she had finished with the ointment. Stepping back, she began to restore the medicines to the bag. "You'll probably have a tender place there for a few days, but it'll heal . . . What all did Adam say about me?" she continued, putting the satchel back into the wagon and returning Tabor's hat to him.

Riley got to his feet. "Sure obliged to you," he said, avoiding her question. "Don't think you should have gone to so much trouble."

Annalee considered him narrowly for a long breath, and then smiled. "No trouble," she said lightly.

Far off in the northwest, in the direction of the towering Spanish Peaks, several vultures were soaring lazily in broad circles, and close by among the loose rocks a red squirrel was watching the activities of the older women with bright intent.

"You didn't answer my question—about Adam," Annalee said, resuming their conversation as she played with a button on the front of her dark blue shirtwaist. Her eyes were even larger than he'd thought, Riley realized, and decidedly a dark brown. But her hair was as he had first remembered it, light brown, almost golden.

"Not much I can tell you. He didn't talk about his—that is, he only mentioned how pretty you are."

He had almost slipped up and mentioned Hale's earlier women friends, Tabor realized—not that it would really matter; Hale was dead and no harm would be done, but there was no need to make public the man's shortcomings— and such knowledge could serve only to hurt the girl.

"We were at the point of discussing marriage," Annalee said, brushing at her eyes—the first indication of grief that Riley had noticed. "There were a couple of things that had to be ironed out, but—"

"Tabor—we're ready for the burying," John McKenzie's voice cut in on his daughter's words. "We're holding up for you."

Riley tipped the brim of his hat, cocked forward to avoid touching the wound in his head, to the girl, and strode to where McKenzie and several men and women had gathered beside the blanket-wrapped body of Adam Hale.

"We don't have a preacher in the train," McKenzie said as Riley took a place beside him. "If it's all right with you I'll say a few words."

"Go right ahead," Tabor answered, aware that Annalee, weeping softly now, was at his side.

John McKenzie began the ritualistic verse customarily quoted over the dead, and ended it quickly. Hale was lowered into the trench and a bit of canvas was thrown over his blanketed figure, after which two men with shovels began to hurriedly fill in the grave. That finished, all turned away and pointed for their respective wagons. Riley delayed McKenzie by laying a restraining hand on the rancher's shoulder.

"Yeh? Something on your mind?"

Riley nodded. "Not sure where I stand—or what I ought to do."

"You mean where Hale's concerned?"

"Right. It's his rig—and everything in it belongs to him. I left Dodge with only my gun and the clothes on my back."

McKenzie gave that thought. Then, "Well, the way I see it, it's all yours now. He doesn't seem to have any kin, at least none anybody knows about—and it could be said you two were partners, more or less."

"You figure I ought to turn the whole outfit over to the law, or maybe the army?"

McKenzie shook his head. "Be a damn fool thing to do. They wouldn't know what to do about it either, and first thing anybody knew the whole works would disappear. Way I see it, you have more claim on all of it than anybody."

"Expect you're right," Riley murmured. Adam Hale and he had been friends, and he had worked with—actually for —the man. Hale had once remarked that maybe they should be partners—a comment that Riley knew had been made in jest.

"Know I am," McKenzie said. "Now, we'll be moving on right soon. Was I you I'd lighten that load a bit. Like I mentioned before, you've got a back wheel that's got some loose spokes. We've doused it good with water, which'll help some, but it'll be smart to favor it till you get to my place."

"Your place?"

"Figured Annalee would have had it all arranged with you by now, bossy as she is. My ranch is southeast of here, once we're off the pass. Be a good place to pull up, check your rig and let your horses rest. Can head on for Santa Fe or on into Texas from there—whichever you decide on."

Apparently Hale had done considerable talking relative to his ultimate destination, Tabor thought. Texas had never, to his knowledge, been mentioned.

"Be a big favor, let me stop over at your ranch," he said. "Would like to let the horses rest, and there's one that needs shoeing."

"Be smart to have them both shod," McKenzie said. "And the rest'll do them good—same as it will you. Expect you're a mite tired of trail grub, too."

"Am that," Tabor agreed, and glanced over his shoulder at Hale's grave. Two men were hammering a wooden marker into the rocky soil at the head of the mound. The crudely carved epitaph on it read:

A. HALE
PENNSYLVANY

McKenzie reached into his coat pocket for pipe and tobacco. "Not much to mark the life of a man, but at a time like this folks do the best they can."

Riley, sadness at the death of the man he had befriended and who, in turn, had befriended him now having its effect, shook his head.

"Only wish I'd known more about him, but he was a close-mouthed man, never did talk about himself. Was my friend, though, and I wish I could've kept him from getting himself killed."

"Way it looked to me, he was dead set on doing it himself," the rancher said, and moved off toward his wagon.

That night they camped along the Canadian River in a grove not far south of Willow Springs. It was thought best for the pilgrims to halt there rather than in the town as it was mainly a hangout for teamsters who were not sparing in their use of liquor.

Annalee came over to the wagon shortly after Riley had pulled to a stop and begun unhitching the team.

"I—I expect you're wondering why I didn't show more sorrow when Adam was killed—"

Tabor, busy with the heavy leather, did not look around. "Your business."

"The truth is we never really got close. Oh, I guess we were together a lot, and I know Adam wanted to, but it seemed to me there ought to be more to life than what he talked about. Anyway, I just wanted to say I'm glad you're coming on to the ranch with us. Maybe we can get better acquainted . . . Good night, Riley."

"G'night," Tabor replied, continuing to work with the horses.

Later, after the team had been tended to and the evening meal eaten, he climbed into the wagon. Mindful of John McKenzie's warning about the weakened wheel, he began to go through the jumbled mass of Adam Hale's belongings, selecting what he felt could be of use to him and tossing what he considered of no value out the rear of the vehicle into a pile. Such would become fair game for any and all of the others in the train.

When he came to the trunk he was forced to break the lock with a small pry-bar, and opening it found that it contained more clothing, as well as a number of books—one by Shakespeare, the writer Adam was forever quoting, several that had to do with the law, and many others by writers with such unfamiliar names as Henry Thoreau, Horace Mann and Victor Hugo.

Placing them aside in a stack, uncertain as to what he should do with them or with the articles of clothing, Tabor continued to search through the brass-bound trunk for some clue that might tell him just who Adam Hale had been and more specifically where he was from.

There was nothing. On the verge of adding the entire trunk and its contents to the pile behind the wagon, Riley paused. There appeared to be a difference in the depth of the box when compared to the floor of the wagonbed. Taking up the lantern, he held it close while he examined the interior of the trunk. Rapping on the bottom produced a hollow sound.

Tabor drew back, surprised and puzzled. The trunk had a false bottom. What would Hale be bringing with him that was so valuable it required the security of a hidden compartment in a trunk?

Picking up the small, wedge-tipped bar again, he held the lantern aloft that he might better see and pried up the false bottom. Tabor drew back in surprise. The floor of the trunk, hidden by the bogus panel, was covered with neat, string-tied packets of currency—thousands and thousands of dollars' worth, he guessed.

9

For a long minute Riley Tabor, crouched over the trunk, stared at the currency and then, rising, moved quickly to the rear of the wagon. Releasing the canvas rain curtain he let it drop into place, effectively protecting his activities from any prying eyes. That done, he returned to the trunk, reached into it for one of the packets of money and hurriedly counted the bills, most of which were old and worn, a few of them new.

Five hundred dollars. Still in a state of disbelief, Riley totaled the remaining packets. There were seventy of them. *Thirty-five thousand dollars!* It was almost beyond comprehension—but could he consider it his? Tabor thought back to what John McKenzie had said, and reviewed the rancher's logic. McKenzie had to be right. What else could he do with Hale's property?

He had found nothing that told him who Adam Hale was, who his people were or where he was from. That he was a lawyer coming west to buy land had been the sum total of information Hale had revealed to him. But did the fact that he had no information on Hale other than that make him the rightful heir to the man's property—and fortune?

John McKenzie, who could be considered an honest, upright man, seemed to think so—which didn't necessarily make it true. But in the slowly settling frontier, truth was basic; he had been with Adam Hale since Dodge City, his only companion; who else could claim a closer relationship?

Both disturbed and elated, Riley returned the packets of currency to the trunk, arranged them in the order they had been, replaced the false bottom and began to reload the thick-sided container with the clothing and books that he'd found in it.

As he did, Riley once again looked through the books for names or papers that might be of help in determining who Adam Hale was and where he had come from—going so far as to even check the pockets in the clothing for such infor- mation—but as before he found nothing but Hale's name on the flyleaf of some of the books, written in a broad, flourish- ing hand.

The trunk repacked, with the books on top of the clothing as he had found them, Tabor continued to straighten out the contents of the wagon, eventually opening the curtain at the rear of the wagon once more in order to discard more items that he felt he could do without.

"I see you're ridding out all you can," John McKenzie said, appearing suddenly at the back of the vehicle. "Smart thing to do," the rancher added, circling the pile of elimi- nated articles. "That wheel will probably hold together with a lighter load till we get to the ranch. I've got a blacksmith there that's a mighty fine wheelwright, too. He'll fix things up in top shape for you."

The impulse to mention the fortune in currency hidden in the bottom of the trunk came to Tabor, and then swiftly faded as several members of the train appeared just beside the rancher and began to poke around in the discards.

"You throwing all this stuff away?" an elderly woman asked.

Riley nodded. "Help yourself," he said with a wave of his hand.

At once several women and children, joined shortly by two men, started sorting through the pile.

"Probably could have sold most of that stuff, specially the iron cookware, if you'd thought," McKenzie remarked.

A half smile pulled at Riley Tabor's mouth. He didn't need to sell any of it; he was a rich man now—at least he reckoned he was.

"Let them take what they want," he said. Then, as the rancher reached into his pocket for his cigar case, a sudden thought came to Riley. Adam Hale had owned a leather cigar case such as McKenzie's, and he'd carried a billfold as well.

"Just remembered—Hale had a billfold in his inside coat pocket. It wasn't with that stuff you turned over to me—and I don't recollect seeing it anywhere else."

"I didn't get to the body first off," McKenzie said. "Were three or four men, teamsters as I recall, that got him out from under the wagon. Was he carrying any money in the billfold?"

"Some. Never paid much mind."

"Probably was quite a bit. Where most men carry their currency—and if that's the way of it, those teamsters got it. Billfold probably fell out of Hale's coat pocket while they were dragging him clear of the wagon."

Riley shrugged. "That means it's gone, then. They probably took what money was there and got rid of everything else. You think they're still around?"

McKenzie shook his head. "Doubt it. They would have turned back at Willow Springs. Usually just take the job of driving some pilgrim, or giving them a hitch over the pass, then head back with their teams. They get jobs going both ways."

"I figure it'd pay to talk to them—to the ones that pulled Adam's body out from under the wagon. They can keep the money. All I want is any papers he was carrying. Could tell me what I need to know about him."

"Probably be wasting your time. The ones who took it wouldn't admit robbing a dead man," the rancher said, and then added: "Not sure I'd recognize them—even if we caught up with the same bunch."

"There any use backtracking to where Hale was killed? Might find the billfold—if they just threw it off into the brush."

"Probably tossed it into the fire," McKenzie said. "Be the surest way for them to get rid of any evidence they didn't want found. I—I'm mighty sorry, Riley. Know you're feeling real bad about Hale's death."

"Can't fault you any. You did all you could."

"Glad you feel that way. Will you be ready to move out in the morning?"

"I'll be ready," Tabor replied.

During the following days, while the Tabor and McKenzie wagons were en route to the latter's Twin Peaks Ranch, Riley's life began a drastic if subtle change.

He had much time to think while the wagons rolled slowly across the high plains country of New Mexico Territory, and at night after they had pulled up to make camp. At Patience McKenzie's insistence he took his meals with them: "Takes no more trouble to fix food for four mouths than it does three," was the way she put it.

That Riley was grateful would be expressing it mildly. He was thoroughly sick of his own cooking—cow-camp fare at best—and Mrs. McKenzie's hot biscuits, beef stew, molasses-flavored baked beans and crisp fried potatoes, to mention only some of the products of her culinary skill, were a real treat.

The only objection he had to becoming better acquainted with the McKenzies was that it threw him with Annalee more than he liked. That she was a beautiful, desirable young woman was undeniable, but knowing what he did about her and Adam Hale chilled thoughts of anything more than just a casual friendship.

Not that there appeared to have been much more than that between Adam and the girl; she had kept the man at arm's length during the entire time they had known each other, with the girl insisting on a hard-and-fast marriage agreement—Riley couldn't remember the expression Hale had used—if she were to see things his way.

Annalee was a cool one, determined either to have her way or nothing at all. And Adam Hale's death seemed to have affected her very little, proving, to Riley's way of thinking, that had she succeeded in making Hale come around to her way of thinking she would have consented to marry him without love being a consideration.

And that wasn't the way Riley Tabor looked at marriage. To him, such was based first of all on a mutual caring for one another—a force that could and would withstand any outside pressure or interference. And it was to be a lifetime pact. It had been that way with his parents, and long ago he had decided that was the way it would have to be for him.

But Riley did enjoy Annalee's company. Almost every day she came to sit beside him on the seat of the wagon, during which time they talked of many things. She had received two years of higher education at the Academy in Santa Fe, and Riley, drawing on his conversations with

Adam Hale during the long miles covered from Dodge City, was able to hold up his end fairly well.

The exchanges served to whet his slowly developing desire for greater knowledge, and he fell to reading from the books that were in Hale's trunk: Tennyson, Thomas Hardy, Paine, Thomas Jefferson and Blackstone's *Law*—these became favorites of his from among the miniature library available to him.

It became a sort of obsession with him to read at least six hours during the day and evening—a program that irked Annalee and brought to the surface feelings that had developed within her while the wagons crawled slowly on.

"Must you keep your nose in a book all the time?" she demanded the afternoon of the last day they would be on the trail. By nightfall, McKenzie had told Tabor, they would reach the ranch.

They were moving across a wide, grassy swale dotted with small juniper trees at the time. The high mountains of Colorado were now well to the north, a bluish-gray blur on the horizon, but the two peaks in New Mexico—Laughlin's and the Sierra Grande, Annalee had told Riley they were called—were still to be seen rising steeply from the gently rolling mesa.

He laid aside the volume he was reading from and grinned at her. "Been catching up on my schooling. Kind of lost out a few years ago."

Annalee, fresh and crisp-looking in a pink shirtwaist and blue skirt despite the many days on the road, smiled in her engaging way and shook her head. Sunlight reaching in under the canvas arch of the wagon touched her hair and turned it to spun gold while giving her smooth, tanned skin a creamy look.

"You don't need any education," she said. "You already know more about things than any man I ever met."

Riley was unimpressed. His newly acquired wealth—the small taste of higher learning that he was receiving from Hale's selection of books—was giving him a different outlook on life. A new world was opening up, one that he was eager to become better acquainted with.

"Haven't you noticed," Annalee continued haltingly, "I mean, hasn't there been a change in you lately?"

"Change?"

"Yes, in the way you feel toward me. There has been where I'm concerned—toward you."

Riley shook his head. "No, can't say that I have."

"Oh, it's those damned books of yours!" Annalee exploded impatiently. "You're so busy with them that you won't admit we've come to mean something to each other!"

Tabor stiffened. He had been careful to make no such impression on the girl, and was actually unaware that she was taking any more than a passing interest in him.

"You and I would go good together," he heard Annalee say. "We could start a ranch of our own. Papa has a lot of range south of the place that he doesn't use any more. I'm sure I could talk him into giving us a piece of it along with a starter herd as a wedding present. He likes you real well, and—"

Riley raised a hand to stem the rush of words coming from the girl's lips. "I appreciate all that, and I'm proud to know you think that much of me—but it wouldn't work."

"Wouldn't work! Why not?"

"Not sure I can explain it, but the way I see it a man and a woman's got to really care for each other before they can make a go of it together."

"And you don't care for me?"

Riley brushed at the stubble on his chin. Over to their right a pair of coyotes were skulking along through the low brush keeping pace with the horses, hopeful that their passage would frighten a rabbit or some other small animal and send it fleeing in their direction.

"Sure wish I did," Riley said, deciding it best to be frank. "You're a fine-looking woman."

"But not one you'd want to marry."

"Reckon that says it. Big thing is, I don't feel like settling down yet. Lots of places I want to see."

Annalee sniffed disdainfully. "I didn't figure you for a drifter."

Tabor smiled. "Never much thought about it, but I guess maybe I am."

"How will you live? Adam said you were just a cowhand. That mean you'll take a job on some ranch somewhere, work for a month or two, then move on? That it?"

That wasn't exactly the way it had been, or would be, Riley thought. He had a trunk with thousands of dollars secreted in it just waiting for him to use. The very pleasant fact was that he'd never have to work again at all!

"Reckon I'll make out," he said, watching the two hunting coyotes suddenly veer off and go racing through the false sage and other scrub growth.

"Yes, I suppose you will," Annalee said dejectedly. Abruptly she turned away from him and looked out over the grassy slopes. "Oh, I'm so sick and tired of my life! I wish I could—"

She broke off abruptly, drew herself to the far side of the seat. "Stop the wagon!" she cried in a high, strained voice. "I want to get down."

Tabor pulled the bays to a halt. Immediately, and before he could offer to help, Annalee jumped down and, head high, hurried to catch up with her parents' wagon, a hundred feet or so in the distance.

10

John McKenzie's Twin Peaks Ranch lay in the center of a broad valley along the north side of which was a line of black lava rock bluffs. Two jagged upthrusts at the far end of the weedy, forbidding formation apparently was the source of the name McKenzie had chosen for his spread.

It was a picture-perfect setting for a fine ranch, Riley had thought as he topped out a rise and looked down upon the place. The main house, a white, rambling, peaked-roof affair with porches running across both front and rear, sat well forward of the dozen or so other structures and corrals that made up the property.

A creek breaking out of a spring a short distance above the Twin Peaks buildings, cut an irregular course, like a shining silver snake, past a small orchard of fruit trees, a vegetable garden, and a wire-enclosed yard sectioned off to contain in order chickens, half a dozen hogs and a cow. The household supply of water evidently came from a well that was close to the back of the main structure.

Maybe he should settle down and build himself a ranch such as John McKenzie's, Riley thought as the horses picked up speed on the slight downgrade. Annalee had said her father had range he wasn't using; perhaps he could persuade the rancher to sell him enough to start a place of his own.

But it wouldn't work, Tabor realized. He would be much

too close to Annalee, and with her feeling the way she did, there would be nothing but trouble. No, as fine as the country looked, as ideal as it appeared to be for raising cattle, he had no choice but to pass it up, and if he decided he wanted to go into raising beef, which on second thought he wasn't certain of yet, he'd best find land elsewhere in New Mexico, or perhaps Texas or Arizona.

Two men on fat, sleek-looking horses rode out to greet the wagons when they drew near. Both rode in close to the McKenzies, tipping their hats politely to the women, and leaning forward in their saddles to shake hands with the rancher. Both gave sidelong glances at Riley but neither dropped back to acknowledge him personally. They would wait until the wagons had halted and John McKenzie could make a proper introduction.

Another ranch hand was standing at the gate to the wagon yard when they drove across the hardpack and stopped. At once two women hurried from the house, both wiping their hands on their aprons and speaking volubly in Spanish as they expressed their welcome.

Riley remained on the seat of his vehicle while Patience and Annalee, assisted by the two cowhands, alighted. McKenzie then motioned to the man at the gate to open the heavy timber affair, whereupon he drove on into the pole-fenced area. Riley, taking his cue from the rancher, followed, halting as did McKenzie at the hitch rack. Coming off the seat, he joined the rancher, who had beckoned to a yard-hand standing in the shade of one of the cottonwood trees growing on the property.

"Look after the teams, Joe—and tell Abe that a wheel on our friend Tabor's wagon needs tightening up. No big hurry. He'll be staying with us for a spell—"

"Don't want to put you out any," Riley broke in. "Probably best I keep moving—"

"Now, I won't hear of that—and the missus won't either!" McKenzie declared. "She's already told Carmelita to open up the spare room for you." The rancher paused, smiled. "Kind of think Annalee had something to do with all this. There something between you and her?"

"No, sure not."

"Too bad," McKenzie said, and turned away, an indication that the subject was closed. He motioned to an elderly man hurrying up from the bunkhouse. "Juan, get a couple of the boys to help you unload. Don't bother with Tabor's wagon. He'll set out what he'll be wanting, and you can carry it in later for him."

"Sí, patrón—"

Men were all about, some hastening to do John McKenzie's bidding, others more deliberate as they went about their everyday chores. Abe, the blacksmith, a squat, hairy-shouldered man with a full, jet-black mustache and thick beard, a heavy leather apron over his stained duck pants, came up to the rancher.

"Joe was saying you was a'wanting me—"

McKenzie nodded. "Tabor here had a little accident coming over the pass. Wagon turned over. One of the wheels loosened up. Like for you to take care of it. His horses need to be shod, too. You'll find a box of shoes in the back of his wagon."

"Yes, sir. Going to take a couple of days—"

"No big hurry. And Abe, tell Ike Forsman to take a look at the off bay. Skinned his leg up a mite when he fell. I think it's all right but I'd feel better if Ike said so."

The blacksmith nodded, pointed at the bow that had suffered in the accident. "How about that? Looks plenty busted from here."

"Fix it," McKenzie said, and turning to Tabor led the way into the house.

They entered through the kitchen, alive with activity and the good smells of cooking food, passed on into a hallway off which doors to bedrooms opened, Riley assumed. They continued on, turning left at another corridor, and came to the living room—a large, spacious area, the entire north wall of which was a stone fireplace. Colorful Indian rugs covered the floor, and heavy leather furniture provided comfort.

"Your room's right through there," McKenzie said, pointing to a door directly in front of them. "Looks like it's all ready for you," he added as one of the Mexican women he'd seen earlier in the yard appeared and smilingly bustled by.

"Place where we'll be eating's through there," McKenzie said, pointing to another door beyond which could be seen a large, round table encircled by chairs. "That other door goes to the parlor. Hardly ever use it unless maybe the circuit-riding preacher, Will Clayton, or somebody like him happens by."

"Boss—"

It was the two riders who had met them as they came off the mesa and down the slope. McKenzie came about.

"Yeh?"

"Asking about that herd we got grazing down on the east range. You want us to move it to higher ground?"

The rancher nodded. "Expect we'd better, first off. However, I want you to meet Riley Tabor. Friend of mine. Riley, this is Sam Lowden—my foreman."

Lowden, a tall, good-looking man, was clean-shaven except for a mustache. He had small, dark eyes and a tight mouth.

Extending his hand to Riley he said: "Proud to know you. Mighty fine-looking rig you're driving."

Tabor nodded, started to explain how he had come by the wagon and team, but McKenzie's voice cut into his words.

"Fellow here with Sam is Pete Taylor—"

Taylor, who was apparently a sort of assistant to Lowden, soberly offered his hand, smiling slightly as he gripped that of Tabor.

Somewhere back in the house Annalee's voice could be heard as she talked with the help. Taylor, a younger man in his early twenties, light-haired, blue-eyed, was also clean-shaven except for a mustache. Dressed in range clothing usual to his work, he turned his attention to the sound of the girl's voice. A brightness came into his expression that Riley did not miss.

"Just like to say," Sam Lowden's words broke the sudden quiet in the room, "that you're welcome out in the bunkhouse, or on the range with me anytime."

"Obliged to you, Sam. Like as not I'll take you up on the invitation."

But Riley Tabor never got around to doing so. He felt uncomfortable accepting McKenzie's hospitality, and somehow guilty in the presence of Annalee. On the third day after arriving at Twin Peaks he loaded up what little he'd removed from his wagon, added the several mason jars of preserved peaches and jellies as well as the lunch Patience had prepared for him, and drove out.

He had thanked the McKenzies for their kindnesses and was most appreciative of what they had done for him, but the urge to move on was strong, and Annalee with her petulant, accusing glances was more than he could handle.

He took the road east. It led to the Texas Panhandle country if he continued on it, McKenzie had told him; or, if he preferred to stay in New Mexico, he should take the right-hand fork at the creek he would come to, and go south.

Tabor elected to follow the latter route, and for the succeeding two days maintained a southerly course, driving slowly while he idly took in the country—a land of bluffs, arroyos, grassy flats spotted with dark green juniper trees and occasional groves of cottonwoods.

Game appeared to be scarce, as he saw no deer, no rabbits or quail, but prairie dogs were numerous, as were horned larks, cactus wrens, saucy scrub jays and the ever-present vultures that soared lazily in the vivid blue sky.

All and any part of the country would be good for raising cattle, Riley thought, passing for the moment through a brushy cut in the side of a low hill. He doubted winters would ever be too severe, and while there'd be no escaping the hot, grass-withering sun, a man could ditch in water from the—

Abruptly Riley pulled in the bays. A rider, gun in hand, was suddenly blocking the road. Two more appeared, each closing in on him from opposite sides. Instinctively Tabor reached for his own weapon.

"Do not draw the *pistola, señor!*" the heavily accented voice of a fourth man warned from the rear of the wagon. "I would not like to kill you. It is better you raise your hands and climb down."

11

Swearing deeply at his own carelessness, Riley, keeping one hand raised above his head, grasped the seat rail with the other and descended. He should have been on his guard; the area was not far from No Man's Land, a jutting panhandle of lawless Indian Territory that was a haven for outlaws.

"Get his iron, Rube," the rider in front of the team directed, motioning to the man near Riley. A thick, burly individual with pale blue eyes and a reddish beard and mustache, the rider sat slack in the saddle while he kept his weapon pointed at Tabor.

"Yessir, Mister Kost!" the outlaw addressed as Rube replied sarcastically, and swinging a leg over the side of the black horse he was riding, dropped to the ground. Older than Kost, Rube was also a squat, heavily built man with a shock of bleached-looking hair and small, dark eyes. A sweat-stained, shapeless brown hat with a ragged brim was pushed to the back of his head.

"Yes sir," he continued as he circled around Riley, and coming in from behind lifted the pistol from its holster and tossed it off to one side. "I reckon I've done that, Mister Kost."

"Take a look inside that wagon, Mex," Kost said, ignoring Rube's snide words. "Expect there'll be something in there worth the taking."

Riley, helpless for the moment under the threat of the

outlaw guns, cast a worried glance over his shoulder. A man in *vaquero* trappings was climbing into the wagon through the opening in the rear. From the restricted look that Tabor could get he appeared to be young, dark-skinned, narrow-faced; and as he moved about, the spurs he wore kept up a continual jingling.

Riley, rigid, hopeful of a break that would somehow enable him to get his hands on a gun, watched the *vaquero* closely. There was little that would interest the men other than Adam Hale's rifle, and the money hidden in the false bottom of the trunk. If the Mexican took it upon himself to open and unload the chest he just might discover the hidden compartment. Riley's thoughts came to a stop. The *vaquero* had thrown back the lid of the trunk.

"Them's mighty fine-looking boots you're a'wearing there, friend. New, ain't they?"

The voice of the fourth outlaw sliced into Riley's fears. Slim, dark, with a careless ease about him, the man had crossed behind the wagon and now was standing beside Rube. He had a sly, narrow face stubbled with gray whiskers, and there was a drawl to his voice.

Riley made no reply. The outlaw, weapon still in his hand and ready for use, moved in closer. Rube grinned.

"Go ahead, Sturges—take 'em! He'll shed them mighty fast if we give him a little help."

"In here there is nothing but things of the *estanciero*—of the farmer," the *vaquero* announced from the wagon.

"What's in that box, or trunk?" Kost wanted to know.

"Many clothes and books. This *hombre* is a *maestro de escuela*—a schoolteacher you would say, I think."

"You for damn sure there ain't no silverware and stuff like that?"

"*Seguro que sí.* I have looked well."

Riley sighed quietly in relief. The *vaquero*, job done, climbed down from the wagon and joined Rube and Sturges.

"Outfit like that cost a pretty penny. Means he's got money on him," Kost said, dismounting and crossing to where his partners stood. Arms folded, he considered Tabor narrowly.

"You aim to hand over the money you're carrying, or you want me to peel you down and take it?"

"Go to hell," Riley snapped.

Instantly Kost lashed out with his pistol. Riley rocked to one side, avoided the blow and then with anger boiling through him lunged at the outlaw. His outstretched hands fastened themselves on Kost's throat, and then a blow, coming from the side—from one of the others—drove him to his knees.

"Hit him again!" he heard Kost say.

Tabor's senses fluttered once more as a gun butt again connected with his head. He fell forward, went full length onto the ground. Vaguely, as if from a distance, he heard the outlaws speaking.

"Them boots—they're mine!" Sturges said. "Just about my size."

"Roll him over—"

Riley felt hands grab his shoulders and legs and turn him onto his back. His head was beginning to clear again, and subconsciously he started to rise.

"Watch him!" Kost yelled, and in that same fragment of time another blow dropped Tabor flat again.

"Ain't no sense killing him," one of the outlaws said. "Just as soon not have some lawdog on our trail for that."

"Hold him down there, Mex, while I pull them boots off."

Sturges' voice was almost inaudible, again seemingly to come from far away. Riley felt his boots being jerked off, and then the outlaw's yell of surprise registered on his flagging mind.

"Whoo—ee, looky here!"

They had found the roll of currency he had thrust inside one of the boots for safekeeping, Tabor realized. He was still dazed and groggy from the blows he'd taken, but he was aware enough to know what was taking place.

"Must be two, maybe three hundred dollars there—"

There was actually two hundred and sixty in the roll. Riley had counted the currency during the long journey from Willow Springs to the McKenzie ranch. The coins—double and single eagles, silver dollars and loose change—had totaled up to another ninety dollars.

"If he's got that much hid in his boots, then he's going to have more on him somewhere else," Kost declared in his deep voice. "Turn out his pockets."

Rube bent over Riley's spread shape. Thrusting his hand into Tabor's side pocket, he pulled it inside out. The coins, shining brightly in the strong sunlight, spilled out onto the ground.

"You was mighty damn right!" Rube chortled. "He's carrying plenty. Maybe another hundred dollars here!"

Scooping up the cash Rube passed it to Kost, and then dug into Riley's other side pocket.

"More here!" he announced. "Fifteen, twenty dollars or so. And here's a mighty fancy dude jackknife. Got pearl handles."

"About ninety dollars here," Kost said, reaching for the rest of the coins Rube had turned up. "See if he's wearing a money belt."

Riley, senses again returning, struggled to break free of

the men pinning him down. Another sharp blow to the head rocked his consciousness, but he was still not out completely, and felt hands pulling at his shirt front.

"He sure is!" Rube's voice shouted. "It's kind of flat-looking, howsomever. Reckon there ain't but fifteen, maybe twenty dollars in it."

"How much we got altogether?" Sturges asked.

"Better'n four hundred here—right close to four fifty, I expect," Kost answered.

Riley felt the weight of the men holding him down slacken as they got to their feet. Head throbbing, vision blurred, body soaked with sweat, he struggled, unopposed, to a sitting position.

"Now this here's what I call a real generous pilgrim," Rube said. "You all best be thanking me for wanting to come this way."

"Reckon we ought," Sturges said. "This here new pair of boots is worth plenty to me. I was damn near barefoot!"

"All comes up to a little over a hundred apiece," Kost said. "We'll just call it even money. I'll keep what's over for grub and such."

"Sounds fair enough," Sturges said. "I'll just take my hundred now."

"Same here," Rube added.

The *vaquero*, sun glinting off the nickel ornamentation on his clothing and broad *sombrero*, said nothing but reached out his hand for his share.

"What'll we do with the pilgrim?" Rube asked, stuffing the money into a pocket. "Ain't smart to leave him setting here. Some jasper just might come along that he'd start talking to, and first thing you know we'd have them, maybe even the law, tailing us."

"Expect you're right, Rube," Kost said, and pivoting suddenly drove another blow to Riley's head.

12

The hot sun bearing down on his face brought Riley Tabor to consciousness. He opened his eyes, closed them instantly to the blinding glare. For a long minute he lay motionless as he collected his wits; realizing at last what had happened and where he was, he opened his eyes again a narrow distance, and moving his throbbing head slightly, glanced about. He was alone. Anger now burning him as fiercely as the driving sun, he got unsteadily to his feet.

A fresh wave of fury washed through him as his feet, protected only by his socks, came in contact with the heated ground. Cursing he picked up the worn-out boots discarded by Sturges and drew them on. They were little better than nothing.

Stamping to get his feet settled, he thrust his hands into his pocket and then probed his money belt. The outlaws had stripped him clean—the paper money he had thought would be safe inside his boots, all that was in his money belt and the loose change he was carrying in his pockets for ready use.

Jaw set, dark eyes glinting, he scoured the horizons for signs of Kost and the other outlaws. There were no riders in sight, not in any direction. Likely they had headed back for No Man's Land, where they figured they'd be safe from the law.

But not from me! Riley thought, glancing into the wagon

to reassure himself the trunk was still intact, and then crossing to where Rube had tossed his gun. He'd chase them clear across Indian Territory, if necessary. No bunch of two-bit owlhoots were going to do what they'd done to him and get away with it!

Locating the six-gun, Riley took his bandanna and wiped the sand and dirt from the weapon, and then, checking it to be certain it was in good working condition, thrust it into its holster. Head still aching, sullenly he turned to the horses. The outlaws had not tampered with them but had passed them up just as they had the contents of the wagon.

Returning to the wagon, he obtained the bucket from the rear of the vehicle, and filling it from the keg ducked his head into the tepid water several times in an effort to relieve the pain. It worked to some extent. One of the bays nickered anxiously at the smell of the water, and taking care of them both he returned the container to its customary place. That done, and hat pulled forward to shield his eyes from the glare, Riley began walking in a wide circle around the wagon. There had been no sign of the outlaws, but they could not have ridden off without their horses leaving tracks.

He found where the men had come in from the northeast —from the direction of No Man's Land—but there was no sign of their having gone back in the same direction. Tabor continued to search and finally came upon the hoof prints of four horses heading due east for the Texas Panhandle.

A glow of satisfaction filled Riley. He still believed the outlaws would strike for the lawless strip where they believed safety lay; they were simply taking a different route to get there. Climbing up onto the seat of the wagon, Riley took up the lines and prepared to cut left and follow Kost and his partners. He hesitated.

Wrapping the reins again around the whipstock, Riley crawled over the back of the seat and made his way through the jumble of boxes, bedding and other articles that the *vaquero* had scattered about in his search for valuables, to the rear of the wagon. He'd not be caught a second time from the rear, Riley had decided, and pulling the ends of the canvas together he tied them securely to close off the opening in the canopy. Doing so would make it much hotter inside the wagon, but he was eliminating the possibility of someone surprising him as the *vaquero* had.

Working his way back to the seat, pausing long enough to get Hale's rifle, hidden by a strip of canvas and overlooked also by the *vaquero,* Riley once more took up the leathers, and kicking off the brake put the team into motion. He veered left, thereby putting himself on the track of the outlaws.

There was no road, no trail, but simply open country. The horses, strong as they were, had slow going since the wheels of the wagon, despite their wider than ordinary iron tires, bit deep into the sandy ground. Around midday, still suffering from the punishment he'd taken from Kost and the others, Tabor pulled up beside a lone juniper tree to rest the horses and eat a bit of lunch. The hoof prints of the outlaws' horses were still definite and easy to follow, but the day was no longer still, that having given way to a light breeze.

Such was welcome insofar as Riley was concerned, for it broke the breathless heat that lay across the high plains and pocketed in the swales and black lava rock arroyos—but it would be unwelcome should it grow into one of the hard winds that all too frequently swept the area. A blow would wipe out all traces of the outlaws' passage and leave him facing the question whether the outlaws had cut north somewhere along the way for No Man's Land, turned south down the Panhandle, or continued on east for one of the larger Texas trail towns where they could have a high time with their newly acquired wealth.

The breeze continued on through the afternoon, making the drive across the rolling, occasionally broken land pleasant, if slow. Riley saw no signs of life other than the birds, prairie dogs, and an occasional ground squirrel in the rocky areas, but he gave that little thought.

The anger glowing within him had not subsided during the long hours, and the determination to track down the outlaws, and reclaim what they had taken from him, as well as repay in kind the brutal treatment he'd been accorded, was still foremost in his mind.

Near nightfall he drove in close to a fairly high bluff, in a welter of lava arroyos, and made a dry camp. After feeding the horses from the supply of grain he carried, Riley built a fire, brewed himself a pot of strong, black coffee and finished off the last of the lunch Patience McKenzie had prepared for him.

As he sat, back to the ragged-faced bluff, staring off into the darkness, he wondered what it would have been like had he taken up Annalee's offer. Things would have gone smoothly for him as a rancher, that was certain. With the cash he now had, and John McKenzie's backing, he would have had matters pretty much his own way.

And as for Annalee—no man could wish for a more beautiful wife, but on the other hand he doubted any man could ever make her truly happy. He was glad he hadn't undertaken the job. On some things the price came too high.

Later, as he sat inside the wagon, all things now rearranged in proper order, reading from one of Adam Hale's many books, Tabor became aware of the wind's increasing force, and by the time he was ready to turn down the lantern and retire he noticed that it had become a howling gale. Making a final check of the horses, luckily sheltered by the bluff from the blow coming in from the east, he saw that all was secure and returned to the wagon.

The wind had ceased with daybreak but it had ended all possibility of further trailing the outlaws. The hoof prints of their horses were no longer visible, all having been swept clean. Riley stood for a time considering his problem— whether to head for the lawless area favored by such men as Kost, Rube, Sturges and the *vaquero;* continue east with the thought they would be found in the new town; or go on as he had originally planned—south—and hope that someday, somewhere, he would encounter the outlaws.

Riley decided on the latter course. Odds for finding the outlaws were now far too long. He could spend days driving north or east and learn, eventually, that he had chosen the wrong direction. Best to consider it a lost cause for the time being, swallow pride and get along with the life he had newly begun. The money taken? No need to fret over that; he had all he'd ever need in the false bottom of Hale's trunk. Anyway, by the time he caught up with Kost and his friends, if ever he did, they probably would have spent all of the cash.

Having come to a decision, Tabor fed and watered the bays, put together a quick breakfast of bacon and several of the eggs Patience McKenzie had included in her gift of trail grub, warmed over some of her light bread and made a pot of coffee. When the meal was finished he loaded up, taking time to delve into the trunk for a hundred dollars or so in currency so that he would have cash for supplies and a new pair of boots to replace the pair he was wearing, and then turned the bay team south.

The name of the settlement was Prairie Flats. A freshly lettered sign mounted on a post at the end of the single street made that evident. Riley, now in need of certain items of trail grub, passed down the dusty, deserted roadway along which a dozen or so business houses and residences stood and pulled in finally when he located the general store. Tieing up at the hitch rack, he entered, made his purchases, and then, as he turned to go, hesitated.

"Did you see four hardcases—one of them a Mexican *vaquero*—go by here in the last three or four days?"

The merchant, a tall, spare individual with ruddy features and tired eyes, shook his head.

"Nope, sure didn't, but it ain't likely I would. Them kind steer clear of this town."

"That so?"

"Yeh, we've got a bounty hunter for a marshal. He don't make no wages, lives off rewards. Word got out pretty fast and we hardly ever see any outlaws or saddlebums any more."

Riley shrugged. He supposed it was too much to expect that Kost and his friends would be on the same road he was following. His luck wouldn't be that good.

"There a bootmaker in this town?"

"Yeh, old man Henson. Find him in his shop, on past John Peer's Hay and Grain Store—if he's sober."

"And if he's not there?"

"The best place to go looking for him is the Yellow Jacket Saloon. Spends most of his time there."

Henson, a slim, dark man wearing a denim apron, was in his place of business. He glanced up as Riley entered the small, cluttered shop smelling of leather, oil and saddle soap, and adjusted the steel-rimmed spectacles on his nose.

"What do you want?" he demanded gruffly as if resenting the possibility of a customer.

"Need a pair of boots. Ones I've got are—"

"Don't have none ready. Can make you a pair in a couple of weeks—maybe a little less."

"I'm just passing through. Need them now."

The bootmaker scrubbed at his unshaven chin. "Cash money?"

Tabor nodded, and reaching into his pocket produced several bills along with the change he'd received at the general store. At once Henson rose, crossed to a shelf on the back wall of the shop, and took up a new pair of boots.

"Here, try these on," he said, handing them to Riley and pointing at a nearby chair. "Made them for a fellow working on a ranch west of here."

Taking a seat Riley pulled off the old boots he was wearing and pulled on the new ones. They were slightly large but not enough to cause any problem.

"Fits all right," he said, "but if they're for somebody else I sure don't want to take them."

"Don't fret none about that," the bootmaker said. "Andy won't be in till the end of the month. Can make him another pair by then. Besides, you've got cash, and money talks far as I'm concerned."

Riley nodded, and reaching into his pocket again brought forth his money. "How much?"

"Twenty dollars," Henson said, a smile now breaking his dour expression. "Sure am glad them boots fit."

"Same here," Tabor replied, and paying off returned to the wagon. It felt good to have new boots on after wearing the old, broken-down, worn-out pair Sturges had left him.

It was near dark. As he settled himself on the seat, Riley glanced around for a restaurant. Hungry, he'd get himself a meal, drive on southward for an hour or two and then make camp. He located the restaurant, The Traildriver, and headed the team for its hitch rack. Reaching it, he discovered the place was closed—and evidently had been for some time. Giving up the idea of buying a meal, Riley drove on. He'd find a good spot farther down the way for a camp, pull up and cook his own meal.

He came to a stream—one, he suspected, that supplied Prairie Flats with water—and headed into the trees growing along its banks. Halting, Riley first took care of the horses, then turned to preparing his supper—slicing potatoes, onions and bacon into the frying pan, adding water and some leftover beans from a previous meal, and setting the pan over the flames.

He had been able to buy two loaves of light bread at the general store, having used the last of Mrs. McKenzie's a few days before; taking half of one he pulled it into chunks and set them on the crescent of rocks that confined the fire, to warm. That done, Tabor filled the coffeepot from the stream and placed it where the water would heat and come to a boil.

Everything under way, he sat back to wait. The mixture in the spider was beginning to sizzle and fill the motionless, warm air with an inviting odor, and savoring it he was glad the restaurant in Prairie Flats hadn't been open. His own concoction would taste fine—although a good, thick steak with gravy and hot biscuits would certainly have hit the spot.

Abruptly, Riley's hand dropped to the weapon on his hip. Off in the shadows to his left a dry twig had cracked. Palm closing about the butt of the six-gun, Tabor stiffened. It could be Kost and his partners: they might have given Prairie Flats a wide berth, and now, attracted by his fire, could be coming to stage another holdup. Or it could be a different bunch of outlaws with the same thought in mind. Drawing his gun, Riley tensed and, whirling suddenly, faced the direction of the sound.

An oath slipped from his tight lips. Standing just within the flare of the fire were two small children.

13

"Where'd you come from?" Riley asked, his voice a trifle harsh. "Scared me some."

The girl, small, thin, pinched face stark white in its half circle of dark hair, edged closer to the boy. No doubt he was her brother—and most likely they were twins.

"It's all right," Tabor said then, hoping to ease their fear. Probably homesteader children from somewhere close by. "What's your names?"

The boy, clad in ragged, homemade overalls and a faded red polka-dot shirt, barefooted and, like the girl, dark-haired and peaked-looking, took a step forward.

"I'm Jed. This here's my sister, Jenny. Mister, can I have a piece of that bread for me and her?"

Homesteader children for sure—and starving. Too many families came into the West—into continually dry country —hoping to make a go of farming, and failed, finding the land and conditions unsuitable for such. Reaching out, Riley chose two of the larger chunks of warmed light bread and handed them to the youngsters. They seized the pieces eagerly and immediately began to wolf them down.

"Your folks got a house around here close?"

Jed, mouth full, paused and shook his head. "No, sir. We're just camped down the creek a piece. We seen your fire."

"And smelled your cooking," Jenny added shyly.

"Reminds me, that stew ought to be about done," Riley said, and taking up a wooden spoon stirred the mixture in the pan about. "Think you can help me eat some of it?"

Jed's face brightened, and Jenny smiled. "Yes sir, we sure could, only—"

"Only what?" Tabor asked, rummaging about in the chuck box for plates to put the food on.

"Pa says we ain't to take no charity. Says it's wrong even if we're hurting hungry."

"Can't call this charity—I just made too much and I'll have to throw a lot of it out unless somebody helps me eat it."

Jed looked at his sister. Six or perhaps seven, he was old beyond his years. After a few moments he nodded.

"I reckon it'll be all right," he said. "Sure don't want you to throw any of it out."

"It smells so good," Jenny murmured, finishing off the last of her bread.

Riley ladled out a quantity of the mixture onto the plates and handed one to each along with a spoon. "Help yourself to more of that bread. I've got plenty more."

Filling his own plate Riley leaned back against a stump and began to eat. He glanced covertly at the children. As they had done with the bread, both were gulping down the stew as fast as they could spoon it into their mouths. Jed finished quickly, looked longingly at what remained in the spider. Setting his dish aside Tabor took the boy's plate, filled it again, and adding another piece of bread returned it to him. Jed said nothing, but words were not necessary; all the thanks Riley Tabor needed were in the youngster's eyes.

"There any more brothers in your family?" he asked, taking up his plate.

"Yes, sir. There's my brother Faber. He's 'most eighteen.

And my sister, Prissy. She's fifteen. Pa says she best be getting married soon," Jed continued with the candor of the very young, "else she'll be a old maid. Ma says that ain't so, that Pa just wants to be shed of her so's there'll be one less mouth to feed."

"What's your pa's name?" Riley asked. Jenny had cleaned her plate and was staring at it with downcast eyes. Tabor gently took it from her, filled it again, and adding a piece of bread placed it back in her hands.

"Zachary Wilk," Jed said, again busy with his spoon. "You want me to take you to see him?"

"Maybe, when you're through eating," Riley said, putting his plate aside once more to add a handful of crushed coffee beans to the pot of boiling water—almost forgotten while he was taking care of the young Wilks. That done he resumed eating, only to stop abruptly.

A tall, rangy man dressed in heavy sodbuster shoes, overalls and soiled undershirt had stepped into the firelight. He wore a ragged-brimmed black hat on his head and carried a rabbit-ear hammer shotgun in the crook of his arm. Behind him in the shadows were three more vague, indistinct figures.

"Jed! Jenny! What do you all mean running off like you've done?"

"We didn't run, Pa," the boy said, coming to his feet hurriedly. "We just seen this here man's fire, and come to see—"

"Come a'begging, that's what you done!" the man snarled. "I taught you better'n that! I ought to whale the—"

"No need for that, Wilk," Riley cut in. "I asked them to eat with me. Fixed up more'n I could use, and it would've been a waste to throw it out."

Zachary Wilk glared at the two small figures cowering by

the fire and shook his head. "I ain't meaning to call you no
liar, mister, but I've got my misdoubts about what you're
saying. What're you doing here?"

"Same thing you are, I expect—passing through," Riley
replied, and pointed at the figures still waiting in the darkness. "Why don't the rest of your family come on in. Coffee's about ready."

Wilk made a slight gesture with his hand and at once the
remainder of his family moved into the glow.

"This here's Nettie, my old woman," Wilk said by way of
introduction. "Boy there's Faber—named after some kin of
mine. Girl's Prissy."

Riley nodded to each. Nettie Wilk appeared to be about
the same age as her husband, forty or so, but she could have
been younger. Wearing a shapeless dress the color of which
had long since faded into drabness, her hair was stone gray
and hung loosely about her careworn features.

Prissy, the fifteen-year-old, was clad in a garment of simi-
lar description but one that had apparently belonged to her
mother, as it was much too large. Pretty, with a tired sort of
resignation in her eyes—blue, Tabor thought—she returned
his gaze with a cool belligerence.

The older son, Faber, was more or less a duplication of
his father—tall, lean, wearing overalls and undershirt, but
no hat. He was darker than Zachary and his narrow face
had set hostility to it that reflected the hopelessness of being
trapped in poverty.

"You called me by my name," Wilk said. "I reckon the
young'uns must've told you. Now, who might you be?"

"Riley Tabor."

"Tabor, eh. Which way you heading?" As he spoke, Wilk
was eyeing the pot of coffee and the remainder of the stew in
the frying pan. Jenny and Jed had now moved over to stand

beside their mother, who was smiling patiently. "That coffee sure smells good. You reckon you could spare a drop or two?"

Riley shook his head. "I sure forgot my manners," he said, and turning to the chuck box dug out the two cups he had. Taking up the pot he filled both and handed one to the older woman, the other to Wilk.

"Plenty more here," Riley added to the girl and her older brother. "But I've run out of cups. You'll have to drink out of a bowl."

"Suits me," Faber said, accepting the small metal container, and holding it while Riley filled it with coffee.

Riley turned his attention then to Prissy. "Got another bowl here if you want some."

The girl shook her head. "No, thanks."

"You ain't really figuring to throw that stew away, are you?" Zachary Wilk asked, pointing at the spider.

"It sure is powerful good, Pa," Jed piped up. "I had two helpings. So did Jenny."

"Probably not enough there for everybody," Riley said, "but if you'll give me a few minutes I'll fix—"

"Let my old woman do it," Wilk cut in, squatting on his haunches. "She's a humdinger when it comes to fixing up a bite to eat out of nothing. Lord only knows what she could do had she a'plenty to work with. Ain't that so, Nettie?"

"Reckon I can—if Mr. Tabor's of a mind to let me."

"Go right ahead," Riley said. "Use anything you want in the chuck box. The bacon's about gone but there's a new side of salt pork. Plenty of everything else."

At once Nettie Wilk, motioning to Prissy, crossed to Riley's supply of grub. She sighed audibly as she began to poke around in the box, murmuring softly to Prissy now and then. Finally she looked up.

"Be no chore to fix up a right good supper from what you got here, Mr. Tabor—if it's all right."

"It's all right," Riley said, throwing more wood on the fire. "Use whatever you need. Eating somebody else's cooking is going to be a real treat for me."

Riley was being truthful when he answered the woman. He could use a good meal, had actually been able to eat very little of the one he had prepared, due to the unexpected appearance of the Wilks. Pouring himself a bit of coffee into the lard tin he often used on the trail when he wanted to brew only a small quantity, he settled back against the stump. Nearby the twins were finishing up the last of the stew while Faber, having taken possession of the cup his mother had used, was helping himself to more coffee.

"Soon's you're done there, boy," Zachary said, "you best rustle up some firewood for your ma. She'll be needing it."

Faber nodded, and gulping down what was left of the coffee in the cup, got to his feet and hurried off into the darkness.

"Where are you folks traveling to?" Riley asked.

"Colorado, maybe even Utah—if we can somehow get there. Come all the way from South Carolina. Been hard on us. Figured me and the boy'd find work along the way. Weren't none. Run clean out of grub a few days back, been living on rabbits and berries, and greens . . . Where'd you say you was heading?"

Riley couldn't recall having said but he thought of no reason to not answer. "South—"

"You got a farm or a ranch down there somewhere?"

"No, just sort of looking. Aim to settle when I find the right place."

"All mighty fine-looking country down there. We come through some of it."

Faber returned at that moment with an armload of wood. He dropped it, paused to smell the aroma rising from the frying pan and kettle Nettie Wilk now had resting over the fire. "Sure smells good, Ma," he said, and moved off into the darkness again, this time closely followed by Jed and Jenny.

"I ain't had nothing but hard luck since we left Carolina," Zachary continued. "Folks out here just ain't like them back home—not meaning you, Mr. Tabor—they're just plain mean sometimes."

"As soon you'd call me Riley."

"Fair enough—and I'm Zach to my kin. What I was meaning, that folks around here don't take kindly to ones that are sort of down and out. They're maybe all gospel-shouting Bible-thumpers, but they sure turn up short when it comes to the Golden Rule!"

"Don't judge them too harshly," Riley said. "There are a lot of outlaws roaming about. Folks have to be careful."

Faber, trailed by the twins, reappeared suddenly, seized the pick handle, and wheeled to retrace his steps.

"Seen two or three rabbits out there, Pa. Figured I might as well get them."

"I'm sure sick of eating rabbit," Jed commented. "Sure wish't we could find something else."

"Best you eat what the Lord provides, and be glad you're getting it," Zach snapped, and reaching for the coffee pot drained it into his cup. "Here, girl," he called, motioning for Prissy to take the container. "Fill this up and get it to boiling again. We're plumb out . . . Yeh," he said then, resuming his conversation with Riley. "We seen four of them mean-looking customers a few days back."

Tabor drew up slowly, his features intent. "Four outlaws —that what you're saying?"

"What they looked like. Me and Faber was hunting rabbits. Heard them coming and sort of hid. Sometimes we get on some fellow's property who ain't exactly friendly. We just kept real quiet and let them ride by. Why? You looking for them?"

"Maybe. Was one of them a Mexican *vaquero*—a fellow wearing a fancy outfit, all silver and such, and with a big hat?"

"Yes, one of them was. They friends of yours? I'm real sorry for calling them outlaws if—"

"Not friends of mine, but I've been hoping to catch up with them. Got a score to settle. When did you say you saw them?"

Wilk gave that consideration, sipping at his coffee as he did. Then, "Was three days ago. Know that for a fact."

"And they were riding south?"

"Sure were. Don't know exactly whereabouts south because we couldn't hear what they was saying too good, but there was something about San Angelo. One of them had kin there, I think it was. Know where that is?"

"Town on the Concho River, quite a piece from here. Was there once. Went with a rancher I was working for to help drive back a herd of cattle."

Satisfaction was flowing smoothly through Riley Tabor. It would be Kost and the others who had robbed him that the Wilks had seen—and they were ahead of him. Luck was running his way. The outlaws, apparently avoiding Prairie Flats and its gun marshal, had swung back onto the main road and were leisurely making their way south. Come morning he'd be on their trail.

"You have some trouble with them fellows?"

Riley nodded slowly, attention now on Nettie and the girl about to portion out the food they had prepared. He wished he could do something to help the family; they were down to bare bones, actually starving if the truth were known, but he knew it was useless to offer them money; such would be an act of charity, and they were proud people. An idea came to him suddenly—a solution, perhaps, to the problem.

"Those rabbits you and your boy've been catching, like to buy five or six of them, and get your wife to fry them up for me tonight. Aim to pull out early in the morning."

Wilk frowned. "Yeh, I reckon we could do that—"

"It'd be worth ten dollars to me. I'll be moving fast and won't want to stop to cook. Having a bucket full of rabbit all ready to eat would sure save me time. Have we got a bargain?"

"Yes, sir, we sure have!" Zachary Wilk said. "Soon as we eat I'll get Faber and the old woman busy cleaning and frying."

14

Everything had worked out well with the Wilks. Zach had insisted on his taking six rabbits, three Faber had killed earlier that night and three from the half dozen or so that were salted down at the family's camp. Nettie and Prissy had worked well into the night not only at frying the rabbits, but preparing other food that would save him time on the road.

He had settled up with Zach and Nettie as soon as the job was done, managing, on the sly, to slip a dime to each of the twins for store candy, and a silver dollar each to Prissy and Faber for their part in the transaction.

Tabor realized the next morning, when he was pulling out in that crisp, quiet hour before sunrise, he had, in helping the Wilks, inadvertently helped himself. With a stock of ready-to-eat food he could now drive straight through, taking time only to rest the horses.

Around midafternoon two days later, Riley spotted a settlement lying in a narrow valley a few miles in the distance, and thinking it might be wise to stable the horses for the night since he had pressed them hard, he decided to pull in there. He had no idea, of course, how far ahead or how close Kost and his outlaw partners were, but felt certain they were still moving at an ordinary pace and that he would eventually overtake them.

Halting at the end of the town's one street, Tabor had his

look at the place—Comanche Wells, according to the sign on a structure that was designated as the stage depot. Locating the livery stable near the center of the settlement, Riley moved on, halting again when he reached the wide doorway of the barn. A hostler trotted up at once to meet him.

"Howdy. What can I do for you?" the stableman, wearing thick-soled, manure-caked shoes, baggy denim pants and an old army shirt, asked. "Name's Ike."

"Want to put up my team for the night," Tabor said, climbing down from the wagon's seat. "Want them rubbed down good, grained and watered—and anything else you think they need."

"Sure. I'll take care of them."

"Place where you can leave my rig? I'll be sleeping in it tonight."

"Got a yard out back. I can pull it in there before I unhitch the horses . . . Sure a fine-looking pair—"

Riley was only half listening. His attention had fixed suddenly on a man coming out of a saloon on the opposite side of the street and a few yards down. A tautness gripped him as he watched. It was Sturges. The outlaw stepped up to one of the horses standing at the hitch rack fronting the place, obtained something from a saddlebag, and pivoting, disappeared back into the saloon—the Sidewinder.

"That be all right with you, mister?"

Riley, anger soaring through him, only nodded. Shoulders hunched, hat tipped forward to shield his eyes from the sun, he started across the dusty street for the Sidewinder. Luck was still with him, he thought with a grim smile; he'd caught up with the outlaws sooner than he'd hoped.

The saloon had only a few customers at that hour of the day, Riley noted as he moved through the open doorway and paused. Two well-dressed men were standing at the bar in the dimly lit room, three more were at a chuck-a-luck cage in a back corner, while off to his right several gaudily dressed women were gathered about a table where a card game was in progress.

Tabor's anger heightened. Kost, Sturges and Rube, with a woman hovering over each, were at the back and the ends of the table. The *vaquero*, shoulders to the door, was facing them, watching as they played a game of cards. Drawing his gun, Tabor swiftly crossed to them, keeping the Mexican between himself and the men at the table until he was immediately behind the flashily dressed outlaw.

As he drew in close, the *vaquero* suddenly twisted about. Riley, jerking the Mexican's pistol from its ornate holster with one hand, clubbed him solidly along the side of the head with his own weapon. Yells went up from the remaining outlaws as the *vaquero* slumped into Sturges sitting at his left and slid off to the floor.

With the sounds of screams coming from the startled women, Riley sent a blow to the head of Sturges, causing him to rock sideways and fall from his chair. Kost and Rube, both scrambling to get clear of the confusion, shoved their women aside and got to their feet, hands reaching for their weapons.

Tossing the Mexican's pistol off into the corner, Riley grasped the edge of the table, tipped it vertically, spilling cards and money to the floor, and jammed it against the two outlaws.

"Go for your gun and you're dead!" he snapped, letting his forty-five drift back and forth over the two men.

Rube, seeing certain death in Tabor's burning eyes, shook his head. "I ain't! I ain't!" he shouted.

"Draw it slow, and throw it out on the floor," Riley directed in a cold, barely controlled voice. "I'm meaning you, too, Kost. Then put your hands up where I can see them."

Both outlaws complied, carefully lifting their weapons from the holsters, and tossing them well out into the center of the room. The barkeeper, his two customers and the men who had been bucking the chuck-a-luck game had all forsaken their places and had drawn in nearer for a better view at the disturbance. The women, withdrawing behind the bar, were watching from that safe distance.

Sturges, moving slightly as consciousness returned to him, opened his eyes and glanced numbly about. Bending down, Tabor pulled the outlaw's weapon from its holster and added it to those lying on the saloon floor.

"Get those boots off!" Riley ordered.

Sturges, now sitting up, glared defiantly at Riley; but as Tabor took a half step toward him, he hurriedly raised a leg and began to tug at its boot. The *vaquero,* senses also regained, was slumped against the wall, a dazed look in his dark eyes.

"Stay right where you are, *compadre,*" Tabor warned. *"Comprende?"*

The *vaquero* nodded woodenly. *"Comprendo."*

Riley shifted his divided attention to Sturges. The slim outlaw with the Texas drawl, having removed both boots, was staring at his feet encased in dirty gray socks that had a wealth of holes.

"Get over there next to the Mex," Riley ordered. "Crawl."

Sturges, face flushed with anger and shame, turned on hands and knees, crossed to where the *vaquero* sat and took a place beside him.

Tabor waggled his sixgun at Rube. "You're next. Get

over there and sit down. Try something and I'll blow your head off!"

Rube, squirming out from behind the table that still held him and Kost to the wall, hurried to where his two partners sat and dropped to the floor beside them.

"What's going on?"

Three men had come in from the street, apparently to treat themselves to a drink at the bar. Seeing the half circle of onlookers they had quickly joined it.

"Ain't for sure," a voice in the crowd replied. "That tall fellow just walked in and took on all four of them others. Ain't said a word why."

Riley half turned to the bystanders. "They ambushed me back up the line a few days ago, took all the money I had, along with my new pair of boots—then knocked me around. I've been hoping to catch up with them. Seems I did. I've got no quarrel with you, so stay out of it."

Holstering his pistol Tabor stepped forward, and grasping the overturned table by its edge, threw it aside.

"I owe you," he said to Kost in a low, hard voice, and drove his fist into the outlaw's belly.

Kost buckled, and a blast of air exploded from his flaring mouth. He rocked forward, arms hanging limply, fingers splayed. Ruthless, Tabor straightened him up with a right to the chin. Kost groaned, staggered back, helpless to resist.

"Hell, mister," a man said from the onlookers. "Leave off. He's had enough."

"I'll say when he's had enough!" Riley snarled, and sent another right to the outlaw's head.

Kost was recovering. The blow rocked him to one side. He caught at a nearby chair, steadied himself briefly, and with blood trickling from a corner of his mouth, squared himself and faced Tabor.

"I ain't that easy!" he yelled and lunged at Riley, fists flailing.

Tabor took several blows on the head and shoulders before he could move away, and then, halting abruptly, drove another straight right into the outlaw's belly. Kost grunted, doubled forward. Stepping back, Riley cast a hurried glance at the *vaquero* and the other outlaws. They were as he had left them, backs to the wall, sitting flat on the floor, apparently with no intention of interfering.

Kost, head low, breathing loud, fists raised, began to back away. Tabor, now sucking for wind himself but not yet satisfied, closed in. Kost pivoted. Grabbing up a chair he swung it at Riley's head. Riley saw it coming and rocked to one side. The chair caught him on the shoulder, splintered into half a dozen pieces. One of the bystanders yelled something, but Riley, unhurt, paid the words no mind. Kost's trick had served only to further inflame his anger.

Rushing in, he hammered the outlaw with hard blows to the head. Kost, stunned, staggered, fell back against the wall. Relentless, Riley bore in, arms working like the pistons of a locomotive.

"Somebody go get the marshal—this is going to wind up in a killing!"

Tabor heard the words this time, but again paid no heed. Sucking for wind, he continued his merciless pounding until Kost, limp, blood smearing his bearded face, arms useless, sank senseless to the floor. Only then did Tabor step back. He stood for a long minute staring at the outlaw as if to make certain the man was finished, and then, breathing more normally, turned to the three men sitting against the wall.

"I want my money—hand it over."

Rube hurriedly collected the coins that were on the floor,

and then dug into his pockets. "Ain't much left," he said
sullenly. "We been gambling and our luck ain't been so
good."

"There was over four hundred dollars to start—and I
want that knife, too. Belongs to me."

Rube obediently handed over what cash he still possessed
—only a few dollars—along with what he'd picked up off
the floor, surrendering Hale's jackknife as well. The *vaquero*
added what he had, as did the still-faced gunman, Sturges.
Riley gestured at Rube as the group of bystanders silently
looked on.

"Get me what's on Kost."

The outlaw turned back to his sprawled partner and went
through his pockets. Facing Riley he handed him a small
amount of change and currency.

"Ain't much. Maybe twenty dollars there. Like I said, we
just ain't had no luck."

Riley motioned the outlaw back to his place against the
wall and glanced at the recovered cash. Less than a hundred
dollars all told—but the amount did not matter. He was
reclaiming what was his, and having the satisfaction of paying the outlaws back in kind for what they had done to him.

"What's the trouble here?"

"Been one hell of a fight," the bartender said, pushing
through the crowd to meet the lawman, a tall, weathered-
looking, sharp-faced man wearing fringed deerskins. "It's
them four hardcases that's been giving us some trouble."

"Fellow there jumped all of them. Said they'd ambushed
him somewhere up the way—and robbed him and beat him
up," someone else close by volunteered.

The lawman, pausing long enough to pick up the guns
lying on the floor, put his glance on Tabor. "That right?"

Riley nodded.

The marshal swore angrily. "Could've come to me instead of tearing up the place, and maybe getting somebody hurt."

"I could have," Riley agreed quietly. "If you're aiming to lock them up I'll drop by the jail and sign the charges."

Kost, beginning to stir, drew the lawman's eye. "You do that," the marshal said. "Just wanting an excuse to jail these birds. Been waiting to hear from the sheriff over at San Angelo. Pretty sure I've seen them on some wanted dodgers. You be around for a while?"

"Only till morning," Riley replied.

Tabor had no reason now to hurry on, but he disliked the thought of having to hang around until the marshal got the word he was expecting from San Angelo about Kost and the others. His presence there wouldn't be necessary, anyway; the marshal would have all he needed to hold the outlaws once charges were filed.

"Don't recollect anybody mentioning your name," the lawman said, motioning for Rube, the *vaquero* and Sturges to get to their feet.

"Riley Tabor—"

"All right, Tabor, I'll see you in my office . . . You jaspers help your friend up . . . Harvey," he added to one of the men standing nearby, "take this gun. Need you to side me while I'm marching these jaspers over to the lockup."

Riley remained where he was while the marshal, accompanied by the man he'd drafted to assist him, conducted the outlaws out of the saloon and into the street. Then, picking up his boots, he walked past the few bystanders left in the saloon, who watched him go in silence, and stepped out into the lowering sunlight.

There were a few persons along the board sidewalks now, as the day's heat had begun to break. He noticed the two well-dressed men he'd seen at the bar standing in front of the depot, evidently awaiting the arrival of the stagecoach. Both nodded to him, and returning the courtesy Riley stepped out into the dust and struck for the livery stable.

15

It was well onto noon the next morning when Riley drove
south out of Comanche Wells. Taking his time, he had first
taken a look at the horses; finding them in good condition
from the night's rest, he sought out the town's lone restaurant and there treated himself to a good breakfast.

Taking advantage of the layover, he restocked his supply
of grub at one of the two general stores the town provided,
returned then to the livery stable, where he stowed the pro-
visions in the box, hitched up the bays, and after settling
with the stableman, left town.

Strangely, he had found the people of Comanche Wells
none too friendly after his encounter with the outlaws, all
seeming to avoid him as much as possible. That Kost and
his partners had been a source of trouble to the town had
been apparent from what had been said, but no one, other
than the marshal, had looked upon what he had done as a
favor. But Riley did not permit it to weigh on his mind; he'd
been in unfriendly towns before, and likely, before he settled
down, he'd be in others.

He continued on south, bearing deeper into Texas as the
weeks moved slowly by, passing through such settlements as
Cotton Blossom, Yucca Flat, Chinaberry Springs, Red
Rock, Kingstown and a few more with like descriptive
names, none of which particularly appealed to him.

Summer faded quietly into fall, the change marked by a

gradual turning of the leaves on the cottonwoods and other trees, a graying of the grass and a decided crispness in the early morning air. But it meant little to Riley Tabor.

He was content to drift aimlessly along, reading from the books he'd found in Adam Hale's trunk, enjoying the country through which he was passing, secure in the knowledge that he had more than enough cash to last him for years, if necessary—most certainly until he came onto his Beulah Land, where he could stop and build a good life for himself. And then, one warm day in mid-September, Riley found what he was searching for.

The name of the town was Sandell. It lay in the center of a broad valley, lush with grass, trees and late-blooming summer flowers. A river—the Feever, he learned later—cut a silver slash along the settlement's eastern edge, lending a fresh, lively look to the area.

That Sandell was an important crossroads was evident from the number of business houses and the activity he observed as he drove down its main street. Not only was there the usual number of saloons, but he noted two large general stores, three or four restaurants, a bank, hotel, stage depot and a newspaper and printing shop.

There were several livery stables, some clothing stores, a bakery, a meat market and a row of offices housing a doctor, a lawyer, a land developer and a gunsmith. Next in line was a supplier of hay and grain, and at the end of the street was the opera house. Other firms, their signs not visible to him, stood along the two parallel streets, while the steeple of a church rose from the center of the principal residential section, which lay across the river.

Well satisfied with what he saw, and his tour of the main street completed, Riley swung his team toward a low, flat-roofed building that bore the sign DONOVAN'S LIVERY

BARN on its façade, and pulled to a halt in the doorway. Three men moving along the board sidewalk fronting the structure paused to consider him intently for several moments as he climbed down from the wagon. Nodding to them, he turned to meet the stable hostler.

"Want them looked after good," he said, laying a hand on the off bay's haunch. "Like to leave my wagon in your yard, too."

"Be a quarter a day extra," the stableman, a squat, wide-shouldered, bearded man in overalls and blue shirt—evidently Donovan—said. "And them horses'll cost you a dollar a day unless you'll be staying for a spell—otherwise the rate will be fifty cents."

Riley said, "Could be I'll be staying awhile. Let you know later." Turning, he pointed at the two-story building opposite the stables. "That a good hotel to put up in?"

"The Sandell? Yeh, reckon it is," Donovan replied. "There's another'n down a piece but it ain't so good."

"I'll be staying at the Sandell then," Tabor said. "There somebody around I can hire to help me unload?"

Donovan, one hand now grasping the headstall of the off bay, turned and yelled into the darker recesses of the redolent, old adobe and wood structure.

"Willie!"

A husky young man, bare to the waist, his bronze torso muscular and hairy, trotted up from the rear of the barn.

"Yeh, Pa?"

"Feller here—ain't said his name—"

"Tabor—Riley Tabor."

"This fellow Riley Tabor aims to stay a bit. Wants some help unloading his wagon."

"Sure," Willie said smilingly. "Where you want your stuff took?"

"I'll be taking a room at the hotel if they have a vacancy."

Donovan laughed. "Expect Linus'll have a empty room all right. You just go on over, pick out the one you want and then yell over here to Willie and he'll start toting things to you."

"What all will you be wanting?" Willie asked.

"The trunk, any clothing you see, and the rifle. Can leave the rest—if I need any of it I'll fetch it myself."

Willie nodded, and Riley, coming about, crossed over to the hotel. When he stepped up onto the porch, replete with rocking chairs and cuspidors and shaded from the sun by a slanted roof, he saw the three men he had noticed staring at him earlier, once more in close conversation farther along the wooden sidewalk. Evidently he resembled someone they knew; to him they were totally unfamiliar, but he nodded as before, and crossing the porch to the screen door, pulled it open and entered the hotel's warm, shadowy lobby.

A small, wizened, balding man with black, shoe-button eyes and drooping mustache, wearing a loosely fitting gray suit and black cotton shirt with no collar, hurried forward to greet him.

"I'm Linus Peabody, you need a room?" he asked, extending a hand.

Riley accepted the welcome, and said, "Like one upstairs and on the front."

"Can give you my best one," Peabody said with a toothy smile. "It's on the corner. You'll get a good view from both the west and south windows. Just sign your name on the register, and I'll show you up."

Tabor entered his name in the well-thumbed book, and then, following Peabody up a flight of steps to a landing from which ran a hallway, trailed him to its end at the building's southwest corner. Unlocking the door which bore the tin numeral 2, the hotelman ushered him into the room.

Though stifling, as the windows were both closed, the room was clean and well furnished with bed, table, three chairs, dresser, washstand and a clothing wardrobe. The flowered carpet showed considerable wear, and the wall paper had yellowed, but on the whole it was better than average.

"I'll probably be here for a while," Tabor said.

"I have a monthly rate," Peabody assured him hurriedly. "Don't you have any baggage?"

"It's across the street in my wagon. The stableman's boy will be bringing it up for me . . . Know of any ranches around close that's for sale?"

"Looking to get into raising cattle, eh? Well, there's a heap of money to be made in cattle, all right—same as a man can make plenty investing in real estate right here in Sandell. I've watched this town double in size in the last five years."

"Sounds interesting."

Riley wasn't looking for any long-time ventures in real estate, however; what he had in mind was putting some of his wealth in a ranch and raising either cattle or horses— but he reckoned it wouldn't hurt to look into property possibilities.

"Who's the best man to talk to about it?" he asked. The room was cooling off now as fresh air began to sweep in from the open windows.

"Ward Preston—runs the bank. Handles real estate, too. I can get him for—"

"Never mind. I'll look him up myself. Where's the best place to eat?"

"Axleman's restaurant is right down the street. His wife

does the cooking, and it's just like eating at home. You want me to tell Willie Donovan to start bringing over your belongings?"

"I'd be obliged," Riley said, and as Peabody hurried off he turned and crossed to the window overlooking the street.

He'd hang around until Willie brought over the trunk and other items he'd named, then clean up and pay a visit to Axleman's restaurant for a good meal. Afterwards he'd look up Preston, the banker, and see if he knew of any ranches that were for sale. If Preston did, and he still liked the feel and the looks of the town, he'd see what the banker had.

Honus Axleman and his wife Hilda proved to be large, portly, ruddy-faced Germans who produced as fine a meal as Riley could have wished. Linus Peabody was right—it was the place to eat. Leaving there, Riley strolled aimlessly down the wide, dusty street, modernized by the sidewalks running along either side, and came finally to the Panhandle Cattleman's Bank.

It was in a small, narrow building with a fairly large front window. To the left was Kilgore's ladies'-ready-to-wear store, while on the opposite side was the newspaper and print shop of one Rufus Snell, according to the lettering on the windows. The bank appeared to be deserted when Riley peered into it, but upon trying the door he found it unlocked; pushing it open, he stepped inside.

There was no one in the single teller's cage, but a young woman sitting at a table behind a polished railing rose immediately and came forward to meet him. Riley stopped short, her beauty and appearance all but striking him dumb.

"Is there something I can do for you?" she asked.

Tabor nodded woodenly, his gaze taking in every inch of the girl. Slim, well built, with dark hair and brows, blue eyes and a creamy tan skin, she was dressed in a dove-gray skirt and a puffed-sleeve pink and white blouse.

"Did you want to see Mr. Preston?" the girl said, smiling faintly.

"Was hoping to," Tabor managed. "I—"

"He's my father. I'm Rowena. I'm sorry he's out for the moment. He should be back soon." The girl broke off, glanced toward the door. "Here he is now. I—I don't think you told me your name."

"Riley Tabor."

Preston was a large man, well dressed in suit black boots, white shirt and black string tie. He had a broad face with deep-set, light eyes, graying hair, mustache and Vandyke beard. That he was a person of consequence was evident in his grandiose, almost pompous manner.

"Papa," Rowena said as he approached the railing, "this is Mr. Tabor. He wants to see you."

"I know," Preston said, hanging his hat on a nearby hall-tree. "You're looking to buy a ranch and maybe do some investing in our town."

Tabor shrugged. "Word gets around fast," he said, feeling the banker's eyes rake him in swift assessment.

Although he had bought a change of clothing in one of the settlements back up the road, he had outfitted himself with the usual, serviceable range wear preferred by cowhands, and no doubt looked to be just that. It wasn't hard to guess what banker Preston was thinking; his prospective customer most likely didn't have enough cash to buy next week's groceries, much less a ranch.

"Not at all," Preston said, leading the way back to a large rolltop desk and several chairs in the rear of the office. "I ran into Linus Peabody. Said you intended to talk to me."

"Then you know what I've got in mind," Riley said, sitting down on one of the chairs. "Not saying I'll buy, but I am interested in hearing about anything good that can be bought reasonable."

Preston bridged his fingers together, frowned, and considered Riley skeptically.

"Are you talking cash or long-term mortgage?"

"Cash—depending on the amount we're figuring on."

The banker settled back in his padded chair seemingly satisfied with what he now knew. Crossing his arms he nodded thoughtfully.

"There's a ranch for sale about ten miles west of here. About a hundred thousand acres. Pretty fair buildings and plenty of grass and water. Fellow's running about five hundred head of cattle. Could be a money-making proposition."

"Why ain't it?"

"Well, man owning it just wasn't cut out to be a cattle grower. Name's Avery Wilson. Inherited the place from his folks—they came here early, when the Texas Republic was giving twelve hundred acres or so of land free to any family who would settle on it, along with the option of buying additional land at fifty cents an acre. Was around 1836. Anyway the Wilsons took up one of the grants, added on to it through the years and built the place up to the size it is today."

"You say there's plenty of water?"

"Enough, but there could be more," Preston replied. "There's a spring up on the north end that feeds three or four stock ponds. The Wilsons dug a well for family use. What I would do if the place was mine, I'd get a team and a fresno scraper, and cut myself a ditch in from the river so's I'd have some ponds on the lower end of my range."

"How far from the river is the property?"

"Quarter mile, more or less."

Riley lifted his glance to the street, caught Rowena Preston studying him intently. She smiled and he nodded, suddenly aware that he was about as interested in the girl as he was in the ranch her father was describing.

"What'll it take to buy the place?"

Preston stroked his Vandyke. "Well, I think if you'd offer Wilson ten cents an acre for the land, throw in twenty-five hundred dollars for the house and buildings, and buy his stock at market price you'd have yourself a ranch—all cash, of course."

"It would be cash," Riley said.

"That would all add up somewhere in the neighborhood of, well—with cattle bringing about fourteen dollars a head, last I heard—nineteen thousand dollars. We wouldn't know the exact figure until we got a stock tally. Could be a bit more, and it could come out less." Ward Preston paused, studied Tabor for several moments. Then, "That be too steep for you, cash-wise, I mean?"

Riley shook his head. "No problem. I'd like to look the place over before saying any more."

"Certainly!" Preston said, his voice and manner now one of enthusiasm. "Wouldn't want you to commit yourself without first going over it good. I can take you out to see it when you've got the time."

"Time's what I've got plenty of right now," Riley said, "but there's a couple of things I have to do this afternoon."

"Tomorrow morning will be fine with me. I'll pick you up in front of the hotel about nine."

Tabor got to his feet and glanced around. His eyes fell on the heavy, shoulder-high iron safe standing against the back wall.

"That where you keep the money?"

"It is. Biggest and strongest safe in this part of the country. Nobody's going to break into it."

His money should be in the safe, Riley realized. Having it in the bottom of the trunk was risky; not only might a lucky thief discover it, but a fire could destroy every dollar.

"Got some cash I'd like to leave with you—"

Preston rubbed his hands together. "Fine. Just bring it over and hand it to my daughter. She'll give you a receipt. It'll be available any time you want to draw on it."

Late that night, as Riley stood at the front window of his room and looked out over the town, quiet now except for faint noises coming from the saloons, he recalled the surprised and pleased look on Rowena's lovely face when he'd brought in his money for deposit. There still was almost thirty-seven thousand dollars of the amount he'd discovered in the bottom of the trunk, as he had used only a small amount—a trifle over a hundred dollars, in fact.

"You didn't rob a bank to get this, did you?" she'd said jokingly as she began to count the currency.

"No, sure didn't," he had replied. Rowena was pleased that he actually had a large amount of cash, that his talk with her father was not only idle words.

He was glad he had stopped at Sandell and was going to make it his home: he'd buy the Wilson place, if it was all Ward Preston claimed, and get into raising beef. Having been around cattle almost all of his life as a working cowhand, he knew there was money to be made if a man handled things right and didn't encounter any bad luck in the form of blizzards and droughts, both of which he figured were unlikely in the Sandell-Feever River country. With some of the money left over from buying out Wilson, he could add to the herd, let it graze and fatten for a couple of years, and then put together a drive and market all of his prime stock.

A grin pulled at the corners of Riley Tabor's straight-line mouth. If he wasn't careful he'd turn himself into a rich man—which wouldn't be so bad, considering the fact he'd never made over eighty dollars a month in his whole life! And he owed it all to Adam Hale—God rest his soul. And he was sure that if Adam was keeping tabs on him he'd approve his buying a ranch and going into the cattle business.

Turning away from the window, Riley moved slowly to the one in the south wall. The night was clear and soft, and the river, like a strip of glistening silver in the strong moon and starlight, was visible beyond the buildings of the town. He could see the lighted windows of the homes on the opposite side of the stream, and wondered which one Rowena and her family lived in; a big, fine one, he reckoned.

Riley's attention sharpened as the sudden, hard pound of galloping horses reached him. Stepping closer to the window he saw riders wearing long slickers and something white over their heads—pillow slips, most likely—crossing the far end of the street as they headed east. He swore deeply. Night riders. Preston had not mentioned them.

16

Ward Preston pulled up in front of the hotel the next morning at nine o'clock sharp, just as planned. Riley was waiting,
and after the usual greetings climbed up into the red-
wheeled buggy and took his place on the seat beside the
banker.

"Fine morning," Preston said by way of starting a conversation. "But that's how it is in this country. Your room
at the hotel suit you?"

Tabor nodded. "It's better than most I've put up in." He
hesitated, eyes on the various storefronts passing as they
rolled swiftly along the street. "Saw some vigilantes last
night. Were headed east out of town. Folks around here
having trouble with them?"

Preston sighed. "Some," he said as they reached the end
of the street and turned west on a well-traveled road.

The air was fresh and crisp, and the sky was a vivid blue
overhead with only a scatter of fleecy clouds well to the
north. Over on the river, ducks were quacking busily, and
the settlement was now falling swiftly behind them as the
tall black gelding Preston had hitched to his rig began to
stretch his legs.

"Some," Riley repeated. "That can mean a lot. Before I
sink money into any place around here I want to know what
I might find myself up against."

"Not the ranchers the night riders are bothering, it's the

homesteaders—the nesters. There are a couple of dozen of them east of here, in what's called Mason Flats. Little two-bit places, maybe thirty or forty acres—people all trying to grow corn or wheat, vegetables and such."

"They having much luck?"

"Very little. This country's for raising cattle, not farming, and the minute they break the sod with their damned plow, they take another step towards ruining the land, turning it into dust." Preston paused, eyes on a flock of noisy crows coming in to the river. "They'd all be better off if they'd go back where they belong," he continued, and then added: "They'd all starve if they couldn't steal a beef from one of the ranchers now and then."

"Don't like the sound of that," Riley murmured. "Can't the law do something about it?"

"Right now we don't have a lawman except for a young fellow who's acting as a deputy. Sheriff died about three months ago. Haven't been able to get anybody to take his place yet. But those nesters won't bother you—they're all east of town. Ranch you're interested in is twenty miles or so west of them . . . Fine country, don't you think?"

It was good country, Riley admitted. Gently rolling and covered with grass that despite the lateness of the year still had a faint green tinge. Small groves of trees were here and there, while off to their left a solid bank of more trees and brush marked the location of the Feever River.

"It ever flood around here?" Tabor wondered. "Land looks a bit low."

"Got to be honest with you—we have had a flood once or twice, but nobody got hurt. River left its banks and backed up for a quarter mile or so through here, then drained off without causing any damage. Helped the grass more than anything."

"How about in town?"

"It's quite a bit above the river, so nothing there was touched . . . Now, the Wilson ranch starts where you see that stone marker. That's the southeast corner. Rest of the hundred thousand acres lies to the right and on ahead."

Small bunches of grazing cattle began to appear, some in the swales where the grass looked taller, others out on the flats and low hills.

"I don't see any water holes—"

"None in this part," Preston said. "Main one is near center of the spread with a few smaller ponds on west, all spring-fed. Think I mentioned my idea of digging a ditch in from the river, and filling up a couple of these sinks. Man did that, the cattle wouldn't have to go so far to water."

"It's a good idea," Riley agreed. "Less moving around a steer has to do, the more tallow he'll put on."

Riley could see the ranch house and its attendant buildings on ahead, the principal structure a long, rambling affair with a slanted roof and a porch that ran its full width; a bunkhouse, a cookshack, a small barn, several sheds and numerous corrals stood beyond it. Smoke was curling up from the pipe stack in the cook's kitchen, and two men were leading their saddled horses up to a hitch rack at the rear of the main house.

A lean, consumptive-looking man with hollow cheeks and deep-set eyes came out onto the porch as Riley and Preston drew to a halt in the yard. The banker made the introductions and explained the reason for their visit. Wilson, his manner stiff and unfriendly at first, changed immediately.

"Just make yourself at home, Tabor," he said. "Have a good look—talk to the hired help, ask them whatever you want."

"How many hands you got working?" Riley wanted to know as they entered the house.

"Only three right now, not counting the cook. Caleb Ferrel's my foreman. Been with me for years, and knows more about the place than I do. Other two are regular cowhands —I don't know their names. Their kind, well, they just sort of come and go. Anyway, I leave all that up to Caleb."

The house was roomy, comfortable, and fairly well furnished with heavy cowhide-covered furniture. The kitchen had not been in use for some time, Wilson evidently taking his meals with the crew in the cookshack. Making no comment, Riley, trailed by Preston and Wilson, passed on through and out into the yard that lay between the ranch house and the lesser buildings.

Tabor had his look into the cook's domain with the kitchen at one end and the dining area at the other, shook hands with the smiling Mexican named Carlos who was in charge of feeding the men, glanced briefly at the remaining minor structures, and paused in the shade of a large chinaberry tree that spread its branches over one corner of the yard. He turned to Wilson.

"Place looks all right to me. Run down some, but I reckon that can be fixed. How many head of cattle are you running?"

"You'll have to ask Caleb about that, but I think it's about four hundred. Sold off a few not long ago."

"You willing to take market value for what you've got?"

Wilson nodded. "I'm ready to sell," he replied in a decisive sort of way. "And if you're ready to buy and have got cash money I'll make you a deal you can't back away from."

Riley faced Preston. "You know what I can do. See if you can work out something. I'm going over and have a look at that horse," he said, jerking a thumb at a bright sorrel standing in a corral on the far side of the yard. "I want him included in the deal."

Wilson shrugged doubtfully and then, turning his head to one side, spat. "Why not? That's my best horse, but if it will help things along, he's yours. I'm in a hurry to get back to Kansas City."

Riley moved on, leaving Preston, a fold of papers in one hand, pencil in the other, to converse with Wilson. Reaching the corral he let himself inside and eased up to the gelding. The big horse, a good fifteen hands tall, did not shy but allowed him to come in close and lay a hand on his neck.

"Sure is a dandy, ain't he?" a voice drawled from the lower end of the corral. "Trouble is he don't get rode enough."

Riley shifted his attention to the speaker—an elderly man with white hair, ruddy face and trailing salt-and-pepper mustache. Dressed in the usual working cowhand clothing, he came forward slowly at a limping walk that bespoke many broken bones during the years he'd followed his trade as a cowboy.

"I'm called Caleb—Caleb Ferrel," he said, extending a gnarled hand. "They tell me I'm the foreman around here. Reckon I am—of what little there's for a man to be foreman of. You wanting to buy the sorrel? Reckon he's for sale. Wilson's willing to sell anything he's got."

Riley, taking Ferrel's hand into his own, grinned. "Name's Tabor. I'm hoping to buy the whole shooting match, if I can."

"Won't have no trouble there," Caleb said, wagging his head. "He's been wanting to pull out powerful bad. You come from around here somewheres?"

Riley had taken an immediate liking to the old foreman and was hoping that he'd stay on if a deal with Wilson was made. "No, from up New Mexico way. Worked cattle up there for most of my life."

"Then I reckon you've got a feel for the critters. This place could do right good if somebody'd take it on that wanted to ranch."

"That'll be what I aim to do. If I get the place, you willing to stay on as foreman?"

Caleb scrubbed at the stubble on his jaw. "Well, yeh, reckon I would. What about the rest of the boys?"

"If they want to work they'll have a job, too. I figured to bring in more stock soon as I can. The range looks like it can handle them."

Caleb snorted. "Hell! A man could double the tally we got grazing here four or five times and not hurt nothing! Why, they's place on this range that ain't never seen a cow."

"We'll change that—if I get the place," Riley said, and turned to meet Ward Preston hurrying toward him. Beyond the banker Wilson was walking slowly toward the house.

"Deal's set," Preston announced, giving Caleb Ferrel a quick nod. "You've bought yourself a ranch."

Riley smiled broadly. "When can I move in?"

"Wilson said it will take him a couple of days to get his belongings together, and make his arrangements—then it's yours. He's coming in this afternoon to sign the papers. You can do the same."

"I'll be there," Riley said, and glanced at Caleb. "You hear what Preston said?"

"Sure did," Ferrel replied, his eyes bright and matching his pleased grin. "I'll pass the word along."

As they turned away to return to the buggy, Preston laid a friendly arm on Riley's shoulders. "Don't make any plans for tonight—you're taking supper with me at my house. I think we're due a little celebration."

"Buying the Wilson spread will be the beginning of an empire for you," Ward Preston said as, near sunset, they sat on the porch of his home drinking lemonade. "Yes, sir, I've got a feeling there's big things ahead for you."

They had arrived at the Preston home—a large, attractive, two-story frame house not far from the river on the east side of town—about an hour earlier. Riley had met Mrs. Preston—Lurah—when she came out on the porch with Rowena to greet him and her husband.

Riley liked her at once. She was a slight, round-faced, scholarly woman with black eyes, graying hair and a friendly manner, and had made him feel at home immediately, but his attention had centered mainly on Rowena. He thought she was even lovelier than he had remembered, with her dark tresses pulled away from her face and gathered in a bun on the nape of her neck, her full brows accentuating the creamy tan of her skin, and the perfect shape of her lips, heightened by the application of some kind of cosmetic. Rowena had changed for the evening and was now wearing a yellow dress with a tight bodice; while very full in the skirt, the dress did nothing to hide her well-turned figure.

Tabor would have preferred to spend the time talking with her, but Ward Preston had business on his mind, and after he and the women had exchanged a few words in the parlor—a spacious, comfortable room with flowered carpet, family portraits in glass-covered, oval-shaped frames on the papered walls, large plush- and brocade-covered furniture, several hobnail lamps and a massive oak library table upon which several books were neatly arranged—the banker had led the way back out onto the porch.

It was a beautiful home, and Riley had found himself visualizing a future in which he, with Rowena as his wife, possessed such a place. But he had discarded the fantasy at once; a girl like Rowena Preston would have little or no time for a common, everyday cowhand like him.

"Expect you're figuring on increasing your herd right away," Preston said, sipping at his drink.

The day had cooled and was most pleasant. Somewhere off in the distance a cow was lowing, and in the trees in front of the Preston house sparrows were chattering as they settled down for the coming night.

"Aim to double it," Riley said. "Man won't make any money with the size of the one Wilson has."

"Agree there. Now, about all of the ranchers in this part of the country do business with me. I'll ask around and see who has some stock to sell."

"I'll appreciate that—"

"Was thinking maybe you'd like to invest a little of the cash you have left over in town real estate."

"Real estate? Figured to ranch, not—"

"Not smart for a man to put all his eggs in one basket," Preston broke in. "He'll have something to fall back on if he runs into some bad luck. Now, was I you, or if you were asking me for advice, and a lot of men do, I'd say buy up some of the land in town, maybe even a building or two."

Riley set his empty glass on the floor. Staring off into the hazy distance he shook his head. "Not sure I want—"

"You can't go wrong on land, or real estate in Sandell," Preston declared. "The railroad's moving this way—slow, I'll admit, but it'll eventually reach this part of the country.

It's bound to go through the town, and property values will go up like skyrockets on Independence Day."

"Expect they will—if it comes through here."

Preston, his glass empty, turned to the open doorway. "Rosa! More lemonade, please."

A middle-aged Mexican woman appeared at once, carrying a pitcher of lemonade. She silently filled both glasses and hurried off.

Preston took a swallow of the drink and leaned back in his chair. "Can just about guarantee that," he said confidently. "I've got pretty far-reaching influence in this part of the country. Fact is, there's talk of me being the next governor—strong talk."

"Expect you know what you're talking about, then," Tabor admitted.

He reckoned it might be smart to invest some of the left-over cash in land—but only after he had done all the things necessary to make his ranch a success. The banker had made a good deal for him with Wilson, and when it was all settled he would still have about half his capital left. But the ranch came first.

"Who's that?" Preston wondered, leaning forward and staring at the shaded driveway leading in from the street. "Looks like Frank Brock, and Rufe Snell, and some of the townspeople. Now, what the hell are they coming out here for?"

The men, four on horseback, two in a buggy, entered the yard and drew up in front of the house. Riley heard the screen door behind him open and close softly, guessed the sound of more visitors had drawn the attention of Rowena and her mother.

"Sure sorry to disturb you at supper time, Ward," one of

the pair in the buggy called as he climbed down, "but this couldn't wait."

"What couldn't?" Preston demanded, rising.

"Come to talk to your friend Tabor. We're here to offer him the job as sheriff."

17

Riley stared at the man in amazement. He—be the sheriff? Coming to his feet he looked more closely at the speaker. Tall, well dressed in a dark suit, a gold watch chain looped across the front of his vest, Tabor recognized him as one of the three men he'd seen on the street apparently discussing him.

"What brought this on, Frank?" Preston asked. "Tabor's in the ranching business. Just bought out Wilson. I doubt he'd be interested in pinning on a star."

"We sure would like for him to consider it," the second man in the buggy—Rufe Snell, the banker had called him—said as he left his seat and came down. The others had dismounted also and all were now gathered at the edge of the porch.

" 'Evening Lurah, 'evening Rowena," Brock said nodding to the women, and then, putting his attention on Riley, added: "Sure would like for you to consider it. You willing to listen to us?"

Tabor's shoulders stirred. "Not saying I'm interested, but go ahead—talk."

"You wouldn't remember it, but Henry Tubbs and me were up in Comanche Wells a month or so ago. We were in the saloon having a drink, you walked in, went straight up to four hardcases that the bartender said had been hurrahing the place, and all by yourself worked them over good."

Snell pushed forward a half step. "I'm Rufus Snell. Run the newspaper here in Sandell. Frank said you handled all four of those outlaws without firing a shot—that you knocked a couple of them out with your pistol, shoved another one out of the way and then beat hell—sorry, ladies—out of the fourth one with your fists. Good story. Mind telling me what it was all about?"

"I told you that, Rufe!" Brock cut in. "He said they'd—"

"I know, Frank, but I need to hear it firsthand. You mind, Tabor?"

Riley shook his head. "No, no reason to. They ambushed me back up the trail a ways. Robbed me and kicked me around some. I had been hoping to run into them again, but figured they'd headed back to the outlaw strip in Indian Territory. Was surprised to see them. Guess I sort of lost my temper."

"Temper!" Brock echoed. "If that was temper then it's sure what we're needing here. I—"

"Hold on a minute, Frank," Preston cut in. "Riley doesn't know any of you. I think he should, before this goes any farther."

"Reckon you're right," Brock said. "Tabor, I'm Frank Brock, mayor of this town. The big general store at the end of the street is mine. Rufe there's already introduced himself. Fellow next to him is Henry Tubbs. Has the feedstore. He was with me that day in Comanche Wells. We were up there on business."

"You already know Linus Peabody of the hotel. Man beside him is Clete Trevison. He runs the stage depot and the inn. Fellow at the end is Sig Nusbaum. Calls his place the Emporium. It's a clothing store." Brock paused, nodded. "Guess that covers everybody."

Riley stepped down off the porch, and going from one

man to the next shook hands. When it was over he returned to his place beside Ward Preston, noting as he did the smile on Rowena's lips when he caught her eye. It was a pride-filled sort of smile, he thought, as if she were pleased at hearing of what he had done up in Comanche Wells.

"We wouldn't have all got together and come out here busting in on your supper, Mr. Tabor, but—"

"Suit me if you'd all just call me Riley. That's what my friends do."

"Riley it is," Brock said, "and first names go with us, too. What I intended to say was that the reason we got in a hurry is that we're needing a good lawman fast. Been without one for some time. Young George Yoakum's all right as a deputy, but he can't handle the kind of thing that happened last night."

"What was that?" Preston wanted to know. "I was in town 'most all afternoon and didn't hear about anything special."

"We didn't either—not till one of those homesteaders drove in a couple hours ago and told us them night riders had hit them again. Killed two men this time and burnt down another house. Makes four places now that they've torched—four houses and four men."

"Things are getting bad—out of hand," Preston murmured. "We've got to do something, that's for sure."

"Just how we see it—and when Tubbs and me remembered how Riley took care of those hardcases up in Comanche Wells singlehanded and without firing a shot, mind you, we figured he was our man—if we could get him to take the job."

Preston laid his hand on Tabor's shoulder in a friendly, paternal gesture. "Well, I expect he's the right man all right."

Brock's attention was on Riley. "You interested?"

"Not sure about this," Tabor replied, casting a side glance at Rowena, hoping to catch her eye again and read how she felt about it. But the girl had turned to the side and was speaking to her mother. "I expect to be right busy on my ranch, fixing things up and such."

"Can set your own working time. Just suit yourself. All we're asking is that you crack down on those outlaws. We need those homesteaders—need more of them, in fact. They're good for business. Can't see why those night riders don't leave them alone. They're off to themselves, never bother anybody."

"We'll all pitch in, give you whatever help you need in fixing up the Wilson place," Tubbs said. "That way you won't lose time from either job."

Nusbaum, a short, heavyset, bearded man in a shiny blue serge suit, white shirt and tie, and small, round hat, nodded vigorously.

"We need your help, Mr. Tabor. Unless something is done the town will get a bad name—and we are all ruined."

"I don't think it would ever come to that," Trevison, the stage depot man, said, shaking his head. About thirty, he was a tall, muscular individual with a full mustache curving down over tight, thin lips. With light eyes and a cleft chin, he was, unlike the others, dressed in ordinary range garb. "That bunch will move on. Pack of outlaws like them always do. Right now they're just letting off steam, having some fun."

"Fun!" Henry Tubbs, a square-built, angular man with sandy complexion and reddish eyes, shouted. "You call killing and burning fun? They've got those folks out on the Flats scared to death!"

Trevison shrugged. "Didn't exactly mean fun. I'm just

saying they'll probably get tired of what they're doing, and ride on."

"That mean you don't think the night riders are men from around here?" Riley asked.

Trevison shook his head. "No, sure don't. My guess is they're some outlaw gang—just like them you tangled with up in Comanche Wells."

"Could be," Tabor admitted, but he had his doubts. For one thing, the vigilantes raiding the homesteaders didn't seem interested in loot, wanted only to burn and terrorize—and kill.

"We're willing to pay you good—a hundred a month and found," Brock said. "Can live at the jail—there's a room in the back—or at your ranch if you like. And do your eating at Axleman's."

Riley again glanced back at Rowena. She was looking directly at him and he thought he read approval in her eyes.

"Be a big help to the town, that's for certain," he heard Ward Preston say, "and you wouldn't have to make a permanent thing of it. Just stay on wearing the badge till you rid us of those night riders."

"By then it'll probably be election time," Linus Peabody pointed out, "and maybe we'll have scared up somebody who'll be interested in taking on the job."

"We ain't sure how many of those night riders there are," Tubbs began, "but we think—"

"Was six in the party I saw last night," Tabor said. "Were wearing slickers and something white over their heads—probably pillow slips. Wasn't able to see the brand on their horses—or even their color."

"Bunch like that's probably smart enough to not ride branded horses. Whereabouts did you see them?"

"Were riding out of town—cross street below here. Headed east."

"Was when they were going out on that raid," Trevison said. "You going to take the job?"

Riley gave the problem a few moments more consideration, and then nodded. "I will—long as it's understood that I'll be looking out for my ranch—and long as I can do the job my way."

"What way's that?" Snell, the newspaperman and printer, wanted to know.

"Your idea of justice may not match up with mine. I figure an outlaw is an outlaw and needs to be dealt with as such. I believe in justice, all right, but to my way of thinking it don't always go along with the law. Sometimes they're not the same."

"Sounds like you've studied law," Snell said.

"No, done some reading about it, that's all."

"Well, whatever," Frank Brock said. "You're the law and you do what you figure's necessary. We want those night riders stopped—however you do it is up to you. That agreeable?"

"Agreeable," Riley said, and reaching forward accepted Brock's hand, sealing the arrangement.

"Good enough," the mayor said. "I'll meet you at the sheriff's office in the morning, and swear you in. Best we move fast. That homesteader who came into town this afternoon with the story of what had happened seemed to think those killers were going to raid them again. Wasn't sure when, but thought it'd be before the week was gone. He'd overheard one of the riders say they about had the squatters on the run and best thing was to keep right after them."

"I'll be ready in the morning—soon as I take the oath," Tabor said.

"I guess that settles it," Ward Preston said then, slapping his hands together. "So if you gentlemen will leave I'll see if the ladies have supper ready for—for the new sheriff and me . . . Good night."

"G'night," Brock responded as they all turned to their horses and the buggy.

18

"Where's that photographer?" Frank Brock, bustling about in the crowd gathered in front of the sheriff's office for the swearing-in ceremony, shouted impatiently. "Said he'd be here."

The itinerant portrait maker, carrying camera, tripod and black cloth, appeared in the doorway of the jail and hurried out into the open.

"Right here, Mr. Mayor. Was just getting a plate ready."

Brock, taking a place at Riley Tabor's side, motioned for the rest of the town fathers—Rufus Snell, Henry Tubbs, Linus Peabody and Sigfried Nusbaum—to form a half circle around them. Ward Preston, not a member of the council but undoubtedly the town's leading citizen, was also invited.

"Put your hand on the Bible like you was taking the oath," the photographer said to Riley as he ducked under the black light shield.

Tabor had already been sworn into office, but for the sake of posterity he placed his hand on the leather-bound book Frank Brock was holding and faced the camera.

The flash powder went off in a burst of blinding light and smoke as the lens cap was removed, and then it was all over. A few cheers went up from the crowd, and several men pressed forward to shake the new lawman's hand.

"I'll be needing several of those—if they're good," Brock told the photographer.

"They will be," the man with the camera assured him. "Been doing this for years."

"I'll be wanting one to send back to the lithographers in St. Louis," Snell said. "Expect to print a picture of the sheriff along with the story of the occasion."

Riley had turned away as the crowd began to disperse, and gone back into the office. Rowena was waiting just inside the doorway, and as he entered she impulsively threw her arms about him and kissed him squarely on the lips.

"Oh, Riley—I'm so proud of you!" she cried as she stepped back.

Surprised, pleased beyond all belief, Riley grinned and, equally impulsive, reached for the girl, drew her close and returned her favor.

"Well, now, what's this?"

Ward Preston's rumbling voice broke in on their moment of ecstasy. Riley released Rowena and came about. Before he could speak the apology forming on his lips, the banker raised a hand and waved him to silence.

"I couldn't be more pleased," he said, "and I'm sure Mrs. Preston will be, too. Rowena has been looking for the right man a long time. I agree that she has finally found him."

Smiling, the girl moved up beside Riley and slid her hand into his. "I know I have, Papa."

Preston, nodding, put his arm about Tabor's shoulders. "Welcome to the family, son. I expect you'll go far in this country."

"Have a big reason to try to, now," Riley said, and glanced toward the doorway where others were beginning to enter.

"We best get out of here and let the new sheriff tend to business," Preston said, taking his daughter by the arm.

"You can see him again tonight when he comes to supper. You'll be there, won't you, son?"

Riley, spirits high, smiled. He hadn't been addressed as such since his father had died many years past. But it sounded good, and nodding to Rowena he said, "You can bet on it."

Caleb Ferrel was among those who had come into the office. Riley drew the old cowhand aside.

"I'll be sleeping here in town—at Peabody's hotel until I get things straightened out. You'll be running the ranch, and the help will still be taking orders from you. Soon as you get back I want somebody to bring in my horse—that sorrel I saw in the corral—and stable him at Donovan's. Then he can drive my team and wagon back."

Ferrel signified his understanding, and repeating his congratulations, departed. Others came in, all anxious to become acquainted with the new—and famous—sheriff, as Rufus Snell had rushed out a special edition of his newspaper that morning narrating the story of Riley Tabor, of the incident in Comanche Wells where he was discovered by Mayor Brock and Councilman Tubbs, who subsequently persuaded Tabor, the epitome of a fearless lawman, to assume the job as the county's sheriff. Another story on the new lawman, one delving deeper into his life and carrying a picture of him, would be forthcoming soon, editor Snell promised.

Young George Yoakum was not pleased at being passed over for the job of sheriff, and he made no effort to conceal the fact. Slim, light-haired, with a thin blond mustache that betrayed his youth, he stood back in the corner of the office and morosely watched the different townspeople he had known all his life enter, congratulate Sandell's new lawman and leave.

Riley, aware of Yoakum's presence, turned to him when the last of the citizens had gone. For a long minute he considered the younger man, and then smiled. "I know how you're feeling. Been disappointed a few times in something I had my heart set on myself."

"Hell, I've earned that star you're wearing—"

"I don't doubt it—it's just that folks figure it took somebody who'd been around a time longer. Now, I'll give you my word on this, you work with me, help me get the job done and when it's over and I quit, I'll recommend to the mayor and others that you take over. I'm not interested in being a lawman, only in running my ranch."

Yoakum's face brightened. He roused, and came forward. "You willing to shake on that?"

"Right here and now," Riley said, extending his hand and firmly clasping that of the deputy. "The sooner you can take over, the better I'll like it."

Moving over to the desk at one end of the small, dusty room, he sat down in the curved-back chair. Other than those two articles of furniture, the office boasted a bench, two more chairs, an empty rifle rack and one entire wall plastered with dodgers bearing the likenesses or descriptions of wanted outlaws.

"You any idea who these night riders might be?" he asked, pulling off his hat and tossing it onto the desk. He guessed he ought to buy himself a new one, just as he should have a suit to wear when he was around Rowena. What he was wearing now was fine for a sheriff or a rancher, but not for going to socials and such with Rowena Preston.

"Nothing for sure," the young deputy replied. "Had a hunch a couple of times, didn't pan out. Been keeping my eye on a couple of saddlebums."

"Any chance it could be somebody local—somebody living right here in town?"

Yoakum's eyes opened in surprise. "You mean one of the merchants, or somebody like that?"

"Smart to take a good look at everybody—"

"Yeh, reckon so, but I sure can't think of anybody it might be—or any reason why they'd want to give them trouble."

"Well, only thing we can do is keep our eyes and ears open. Meantime, I want you to ride out and talk to those homesteaders on the Flats. Tell them to have a rider all set to come to town in a hurry the minute those vigilantes show up, and let us know. You'll be sleeping here at the jail—I'll be in my room at the hotel."

"You wanting me to move in here?" Yoakum said, frowning.

"Right. It'll be only till we nail that bunch, then I'll be going out to my ranch to stay, and you can do whatever you like, keep on living here or go back to where you've been. You'll be the sheriff and it'll be your decision. Main thing is we've both got to be available on quick notice if we're to put an end to those night riders."

"Yes, sir," George Yoakum said with a broad smile. "I'll get started at what you want done right away!" And pivoting, he hurried out of the office.

Riley spent the next hour rearranging and dusting the office, going through the desk, and having a look at the two iron-barred cells which appeared to have been used but little in the past months. He ate no lunch, and after paying a visit to Sig Nusbaum's clothing store and ordering the suit he had in mind, he borrowed a horse from Red Donovan, necessary since Ferrel had not as yet sent in the sorrel, and rode about town taking in its alleys and byways as well as its outlying surroundings so as to thoroughly familiarize himself with his territory.

Around midafternoon Deputy Yoakum returned, reporting that the plan Riley had set forth was in operation; that at the first sign of the night riders a messenger would be on his way to town. That matter settled, Tabor met Ward Preston at the bank where he signed the papers that made the ranch his, and then rode on to the banker's home where he was again to be a guest for supper.

Rowena and her mother met him at the door, the girl welcoming Riley with a kiss while Lurah Preston looked on smiling.

"I was so pleased when I heard," she said. "At first I thought perhaps it had all happened too quickly, but Rowena assured me that it had not—that she knew you were the one for her when you came into the bank that first day."

"Kind of think it was mutual then," Riley said, and glanced back over his shoulder. Ward Preston was just turning into the drive.

"I know you'll both be very happy," the older woman continued, and stepped out onto the porch to greet her husband.

"Glad you're already here," Preston said, nodding to Riley as he came through the doorway. "Want to talk to you about some real estate."

Rowena's brow puckered. "Can't that wait till after supper, Papa?"

"Could, but I figure Riley would like to hear about it now—and I wanted to tell him first off that I located a block of ten lots right here in town. Can buy up the whole plot for less than two thousand dollars. How's that sound?"

"Good—if you think so—"

"That's not all. The building where Doc Winters and the

others have their offices—four places—you can buy for twenty-five hundred. It's bringing in good rent every month. Twelve-fifty from each one of them. My advice is to snap up both deals."

Riley shrugged. "If you think it's a good idea, go ahead. Just be sure I've got enough left to buy some cattle and run my ranch on."

"You'll have more than enough, don't fret about that— and don't forget you'll be raking in a good salary as sheriff from now on, too."

That evening spent with Rowena and her parents was most pleasant and enjoyable, as were those that followed. He made plans with Rowena, talked with Ward about the past and future of Sandell and the country in general, and spent considerable time discussing the books he had read with Lurah Preston. She would have had much in common with Adam Hale, he realized.

He had gotten a little behind with his own reading, what with his new responsibilities and the time devoted to Rowena at her parents' home—and near the end of that first week after taking office, he decided to stay up at least one hour before retiring and catch up.

He had just settled down the second night after putting his plan into effect when he heard a rider enter the street at a hard gallop. Rising, Tabor went to his window and glanced out. A horse was standing in front of the jail. It could mean only one thing; the night riders had struck again. Hastily strapping on his gun, Riley pulled on his hat and started for the door. In that same moment he heard George Yoakum's voice as the deputy came pounding up the stairs.

"Sheriff! Them killers are raiding the homesteaders again! Word just come."

19

The boy, barefooted, no shirt, wearing only a pair of faded, patched overalls, was twelve, perhaps thirteen years of age. His name was Vinnie.

"There's seven of them, Sheriff!" he said, eyes glowing with excitement as he waited for Riley to throw a saddle and bridle on the sorrel stabled at Donovan's. "I reckon they're the same as before."

"They wearing slickers like before?" Yoakum wanted to know.

"Yep, slickers and them white things over their heads. Pillow slips, I expect they are."

Tabor pulled the saddle's cinch tight and tucked the surplus leather in under the buckle. As he swung up onto the sorrel he turned to Vinnie. The boy, riding bareback, was already aboard the small white mare he was using.

"When we get close to where they are I want you to drop back, and stay out of the way. Understand?"

"I can shoot a gun!" Vinnie declared stoutly. "You just loan me a old double-barrel and I'll—"

"That'd be about the quickest way I know of for you to get yourself shot," Riley said sternly. "Those night riders are all killers—probably hired gunmen. They'd blow your head off before you could cock a hammer. You did your part coming after us."

Vinnie stirred in disappointment as they rode out of the

stable. Donovan had not put in an appearance while they were getting the sorrel, which pleased Riley. He didn't want the men of the town, alerted by the stableman, volunteering to become a posse. Such parties were generally more trouble than they were worth unless all happened to be experienced law officers.

"You lead the way," Riley said, motioning to the boy. "I want to come in on them from behind."

"Yes, sir, Sheriff," the boy answered, and broke his pony into a lope. "Sure do wish you'd give me a gun though, so's I could help."

Riley made no reply, and with Deputy Yoakum an arm's length to his left, followed the boy out of town and into the low, brushy hills to the east. They rode steadily for a good quarter hour; then, hearing the faint popping sound of guns in the distance and as a red glow began to show on the horizon, Tabor increased the pace.

Shortly they reached the first of the homesteads on Mason Flats, a low-roofed hut squatting at the fore end of a garden. To its left were makeshift yards in which were a cow, a horse and the indication of chickens. No lights showed in the windows of the house, but a bearded man, white hair shining in the moonlight, and wearing only undershirt and pants undoubtedly donned hastily, stood at the corner of the hut, a long-barreled rifle in his hands. He whirled to meet Riley and the others as they rode up.

"It's me—Vinnie Carson, Mr. Lee!" the boy yelled. "I'm a'bringing the sheriff and the deputy. They're going after them killers!"

Lee relaxed. "About time somebody was doing something," he grumbled, pointing to the glow. "Looks like they're burning down the Lockwood place this time. If they come back this way I aim—"

Riley was pulling away. The red glare of the fire was all he needed to direct him, and with Yoakum following closely he put the big sorrel into a lope and began to follow a shallow curve designed to bring him up to the fire from the hills to the north.

They rode fast, passing several of the homesteaders' places, and when they came to what appeared to be the last before reaching Lockwood's, Riley waved Vinnie Carson to a halt.

"You wait here," he said, and as the boy slowed and drew off turned to the deputy. "This your first time at a showdown like this?"

"First time," Yoakum admitted.

"Kind of figured that. I've got only one thing to say: if you have to throw down on one of those outlaws—and you best figure you will—pull the trigger. Don't wait to see what he's going to do because he sure as hell is going to kill you. He won't hold back."

The deputy nodded woodenly. "I ain't never killed a man —never even shot at one—"

Riley shook his head. "Can hope you won't ever have to, but if you're going to wear a star you better get used to the idea."

"Never wanted to be nothing else but a lawman—"

"Expect you'll get an idea today of what it's like to be one," Riley said, guiding the sorrel through a stand of mesquite. "Big thing is keep your wits—and watch your hind side."

The shooting grew louder as they drew near the Lockwoods', and then ceased as they reached the low hills nearby. The glow of the fire had dulled, but the air was filled with the smell of wood smoke larded with the odors of burning clothing, bedding and other things the house had contained.

"I can see them," Yoakum said suddenly, pointing. "They've pulled up in the yard and are talking to the Lockwoods. There's somebody laying on the ground."

Riley had moved to where he could follow the line of the deputy's leveled finger. At once he veered the sorrel hard right, and rode quietly in to the rear of a small shed the outlaws had not bothered to torch, where he drew to a halt. Dismounting, drawing his gun, and motioning for George Yoakum to do the same, he worked his way in through the smoke and shadows until he and the deputy were only ten yards or so behind the outlaws.

"Want this to be the last goddam time we come here!" the man slightly out in front of the other masked riders said, shifting on his saddle. "You squatters ain't welcome in this country—and you'd best move on or we'll see that you do."

"We ain't a'going," a lanky youngster in overalls stated flatly.

"Better think that over," the masked man said, and pointed to the prone figure on the ground. "Unless you all want to end up like him."

The dead man apparently was Lockwood himself. The woman, three small children and the older boy who had spoken up were evidently his family.

"You pass the word along—this here's our last warning. Get off the Flats and stay off. Made that clear to them other nesters but the rest of you didn't seem to catch on. Now, I want you gone—every goddam one of you—"

"What you're going to get is a rope," Riley cut in quietly, and cocked his forty-five.

In the abrupt hush that followed, George Yoakum also

drew back the hammer of his weapon, the sound abnormally loud in the smoke-filled night.

"Every damn one of you put your right hand up over your head, then come off the saddle. Any one of you that's got a different idea is asking for a bullet."

There was a long moment of hesitation on the part of the masked outlaws, and then all began to dismount. On the ground they stood motionless. The only sounds to be heard were the crackling and popping of the dwindling fires and the weeping of one of the children.

"Turn around—slow—"

At Tabor's order the outlaws began to slowly comply. Midway, the man near the center suddenly threw himself to one side. His hand came up fast, gun glinting in the eerie light. Riley triggered his weapon, saw the outlaw lurch and start to fall. Two more of the masked riders—the one who had been doing the talking and another close by—spun. Both had their guns up and ready.

"Look out!"

Riley shouted a warning at the deputy as he triggered his weapon at the outlaw throwing down on him, but Yoakum seemed frozen, unable to move. Tabor's bullet knocked the outlaw leveling at him to his knees. Instantly he pivoted, fired at the leader of the night riders. He was a fraction of time too late. His bullet had struck the outlaw a moment after the man had driven a leaden slug into the young deputy. Through the drifting clouds of pungent powder smoke, Riley watched Yoakum sink slowly and fall forward—almost head to head with the leader of the night riders.

Throwing a warning glance at the three remaining outlaws, Riley walked to where Yoakum lay. Picking up the deputy's weapon and thrusting it under his belt, he searched Yoakum's wrist for a pulse. There was none. Anger racing through him, he crossed to the fallen outlaws, briefly examined them. They were dead also. Turning then to the remaining masked men, now standing rigidly, arms stretched above their heads, he relieved them of their weapons.

"One of you get me some rope," he called in a barely controlled voice to the Lockwoods.

The older boy started off for what had evidently been a barn. He halted abruptly. The building was little more than smoldering ashes. Only then did Tabor realize the family probably had nothing at all left.

"There's a rope on my saddle," he said, pointing to the shed at the lower end of the yard. "Be obliged to you if you'll bring up both of the horses, too."

Young Lockwood turned obediently to do what he was bid. Nearby Mrs. Lockwood was bending over the body of her husband. Dry-eyed, she was stroking the man's slack face tenderly.

"I ought to blow your damned heads off—all of you," Riley said, grinding out the words. "You see what you've done to this family—folks who never hurt any of you!"

"We was getting paid for hurrahing them, and maybe doing some burning. Weren't going to be no killings," one of the masked men said.

"Pull off those damned masks so's I can see you!" Riley snarled. "Who paid you?"

The three outlaws, features now visible, pointed to the man who had slain George Yoakum. "Him. He's the boss. Was him ramrodding things."

Gun still covering the outlaws, Riley crossed to where the night rider leader lay. Bending down he hooked a finger in one of the eye holes cut in the pillow slip and jerked it off. A curse slipped from Riley's tight lips. It was Clete Trevison, the owner of the stage depot.

"Him!" Riley muttered, rising. "Why the hell would he get mixed up in something like this?"

"The railroad," one of the outlaws replied.

Riley had not expected an answer. The question had been purely in surprised reaction. He turned to the rider, a short, heavy-set, black-bearded man. "What about the railroad?"

"He had a partner back east somewheres that's in with the high muckity-mucks that run things. Told Clete where the railroad would be laying tracks. It'll be right across this here flats. Trevison had to clear the nesters off so's he could put in a claim for the land. Then him and his partner could clean up big."

20

The stunning surprise and shock that rocked Sandell when it became known that Clete Trevison was the leader of the night riders was overshadowed only by the sadness felt at the death of young deputy sheriff George Yoakum.

At the cemetery, while long-faced Thomas Drayle, minister of the local church, tall and forbidding-looking in a swallowtail coat and razor-sharp creased trousers, spoke the final words necessary at the committal, Riley felt a tremor of remorse pass through him. Rowena, at his side and holding to his arm, pressed it reassuringly.

"It wasn't your fault," she murmured. "You've got to stop blaming yourself."

Riley shook his head and glanced about at the three dozen or so persons attending the service. Trevison had already been buried, as had the two other outlaw marauders.

"I told him to be careful—warned him to shoot first, not think about it. Can't help feeling responsible for him getting killed."

"You did all you could," Rowena said. "He wanted to be a lawman and I'm sure he knew what he'd be up against."

Later, as he walked slowly back to town with Rowena and her parents, Preston brushed aside all of Riley's regrets.

"Can't fault yourself for him getting killed, son. Was the way it was meant to be . . . While we're all together there's something I'd like to talk over. Where were you planning to go?"

"Was aiming to rent a buggy and take Rowena for a drive along the river," Riley answered. "Got to get a few things in my mind sorted out."

"I can understand, but first I've got a proposition for you. Somebody's got to keep the stagecoach depot going. I don't know who owns it—somebody back in Missouri, I think. I propose that you and I each put up five hundred dollars in escrow as buyers, and take it over. We can hire a man to run it for us."

"It's all right with me," Tabor said, indifferently.

"I'll make a trip back to Missouri soon as I can find out who the stage line's owners are, get the matter settled. Also, I intend to look into the matter of the railroad, see when they expect to reach here and find out exactly where they expect to lay the rails."

"Anything you do is jake with me," Riley said, not particularly interested in talking business. All he wanted was to be alone with Rowena, but felt he did owe Ward Preston the courtesy of listening.

They reached the bank, where Ward and Lurah turned off. Riley having assured the banker and his wife that he would be at the family home that night for supper, he and Rowena continued on their way.

"I'm getting to be a regular boarder at your home," he commented as they drew near Donovan's stables. "Feel like I ought to start paying for my meals."

"You're part of the family," the girl said. "At least I hope you will be."

Riley drew to a halt. Taking Rowena by the shoulders he faced her squarely. "I reckon that gives me the chance I've been looking for—the chance to ask you a question."

"Question? About what?"

"Just this—will you marry me? Know we've sort of thought about it but I never did come right out and ask you."

Rowena, smiling brightly, tears sparkling in her eyes, nodded.

"Haven't got a whole lot to offer you yet, but I'll work hard at it, and I'll give you everything I can—and I'll cherish you and always be good to you. If—"

Rowena placed a finger against his lips to silence his words. "Of course I'll marry you, Riley. And whether you have anything or not wouldn't matter. All that counts is that you love me."

"No need to even ask that! Never thought anybody could ever mean so much to me as you do. But what about your folks? Know your pa likes me but I'm not sure he'll welcome me as a son-in-law."

"He'll be pleased—he looks on you as the son he never had. And Mama, well, she sort of fell in love with you the first time she saw you—just like I did. I'm surprised you didn't realize how we all felt. Even Rosa, our cook, likes you—*un caballero fino,* she said.

Riley shook his head. "Never was any hand to take things for granted," he said, relief in his voice. "Good to know how you and your folks feel."

"We'll tell them tonight at supper—"

"Fine. How soon can we get married?"

"Oh, Mama will want to have a big church affair. So will Papa. He'll invite everybody in this part of the state. I expect we'd best plan on it being a June wedding."

"June!" Tabor echoed in a falling voice. "That's a long time off! I'd like for it to be tomorrow—but I reckon if I've waited this long, I can wait a little longer."

"It couldn't be as long as you made it sound. We've only known each other for a short time!"

"Maybe so, but it sure will be hard to wait for June—"

"Sheriff—"

Riley and Rowena again halted. Rufus Snell was hurrying up the street to meet them.

"Wanted to tell you I'm getting out a special edition about Trevison and those other outlaws, and how you brought them down. Just wish that plate would get here from that lithograph company so's I could print your picture along with the story."

"As soon you didn't play it up all that much. Were some men killed and—"

"Why not make a big to-do about it? It'll be good for this town. Shows we've got a man here who can keep law and order. Besides, the publicity will do you good."

Tabor shrugged. "Why would I want publicity?"

The newspaper editor grinned, glanced off in the direction of Henry Brock's store. "Heard the mayor talking with some of the folks—ranchers, other businessmen and the like. They think you deserve a bigger office than sheriff—the district judge."

Riley's jaw sagged. "Me—a judge? I'm no lawyer, never even—"

"Common sense is all a man needs to be a district judge. And you've done a lot of studying—we've all seen you reading. I remember Ward saying he saw a law book on the table in your room—Blackstone, he said it was."

"Read from it some, sure, same as I have from a lot of other books. But that don't mean I—"

"Just keep what I said in mind," Snell broke in. "Brock and the rest of the town council will likely talk to you about it one of these days . . . I just wanted you to know about the paper. I'll be printing more when the plate gets here. Got a great idea for the story—about you, the kind of lawman who tamed the West."

Snell turned away and headed for his office while Riley, Rowena on his arm, continued on his way.

"It would be wonderful," the girl mused, "if you got to be a judge and Papa became the governor."

"I'm flat out not interested in being a judge," Tabor said bluntly. "I want to start working my ranch, not hiring it done. And I can't do that until I find somebody who'll take over the job as sheriff. Sure couldn't be a rancher if I was a judge." He drew to a halt as they reached Donovan's livery barn. "Will it make a difference to you if I turned the offer down?"

"Of course not!" Rowena replied indignantly. "I want what you want."

Riley heaved a sigh of relief. "Sure glad to hear that," he said as they turned into the stable's runway.

Donovan and his son came forward at once to greet them. "Howdy Miss Preston, howdy Sheriff. I reckon you're after the rig you was talking to me about."

Riley nodded. "Like to take it out."

Donovan turned to his son. "Hitch up that pair of blacks to the buggy that fellow brought in a few days ago. The sheriff fancies buying the outfit."

Young Donovan hurried back into the depths of the barn, filled with the rank smells of hay, horse droppings and leather.

"Them bays of yours doing all right?" the stableman asked.

"Doing fine. Ferrel's using them some out at the ranch to keep them from getting fat and lazy."

"Sure a real good team—and that wagon. Had a chance

to look it over when it was here. I'm betting it cost a pretty penny!"

"Red's talking about the rig I had when I came here. It's out at the ranch now."

"Mighty fine outfit all right," Donovan assured Rowena, "but you just wait till you see the span of blacks and the buggy he's aiming to buy . . . They're a-coming now."

Rowena gasped when she looked at the team and the shiny new buggy that the younger Donovan brought into the runway and halted.

"They're beautiful—and that buggy, it's—"

"Can say it's my wedding present to you," Riley whispered. "Figured to give it to you the day we got married—but since June's a fair piece off it'll come a bit ahead of time."

"That doesn't matter—it means just as much," Rowena said happily. "Come on—let's take a ride in it right now."

The winter months—sunny, cold days and windy nights —set in. Snow seldom fell on Sandell and it did not that year, leaving both Christmas and New Year's Day to be celebrated without benefit of the white flakes.

As plans for the wedding progressed, Riley located and hired a deputy who he felt could handle the job as sheriff when the time came for him to resign. Meanwhile Rufe Snell received the long-awaited likeness of Tabor and printed his picture along with the planned article he had mentioned—one that extolled the virtues and abilities of Sandell's lawman, the exemplification of an honest, dedicated officer and one that all other wearers of the star could well emulate, in the editor's glowing words.

Riley took considerable, good-natured ribbing over the printed piece but reckoned it wouldn't hurt, that it actually might cut down the number of saddlebums and tramps that were tempted to find a roost in the town, and perhaps even turn aside a few of the hardened outlaws who were roaming the country.

During those months he was able to add to his herd, buying up stock with the aid of Ward Preston, in small jags of fifty and a hundred head, usually at a very low cost from ranchers who were feeling the need for immediate cash rather than waiting for summer to make a drive to market.

Caleb Ferrel ran the ranch as if it were his own, and while it had become necessary to hire two more cowhands at a cost of forty dollars a month and found, Riley knew the place was making money and by that time was worth at least a third more than he'd paid for it.

And then on the first of May, as he stood in his office speaking with Preston, Frank Brock and Henry Tubbs about the need to add another deputy to the force due to the number of persons moving into the area in response to editor Snell's article, the stagecoach brought in a distinctly different stranger.

Dressed in a well-tailored broadcloth business suit, white shirt and bow tie, polished shoes, and a narrow-brimmed hat, he was as out of place on the dusty streets of Sandell as a burro in a corral of racehorses.

"Easterner," Preston guessed. "New York, I'd say."

"Or Boston," Brock suggested, and added: "Reckon we'll mighty quick know which. He's headed this way."

The stranger crossed the street to the sheriff's office and entered. Nodding curtly to the three men, he said: "I'm looking for a man named Tabor—Riley Tabor. Expect you know him."

There was a sharp impatience in the man's tone, and his

small, dark eyes set deep below overhanging brows were hard-surfaced.

"We might," Brock said, equally crisp.

"My name's William Johnson. I'm a lawyer," the stranger continued, and put his level gaze on Riley. "Are you Tabor? He was said to be a lawman."

"I am. What can I do for you?"

Johnson reached into his inside coat pocket, drew forth a fold of papers. "Here are my credentials. I represent the Ohio River Community Association," he said. "I want the thirty-seven thousand dollars you took off the dead body of Adam Hale."

21

"What's that?" Ward Preston demanded sharply. "What's that about him taking money off a dead body?"

Johnson nodded. Several persons moving along the wooden walk nearby, attracted by Preston's half-shouted question, paused to look on and listen curiously.

"Tabor was with a man named Adam Hale who represented a group of farm people back in Ohio. A few years back they decided to move west, start their lives over."

"Could be you've got your man mixed up," Frank Brock said. "Know for a fact that Riley Tabor's from the upper part of New Mexico Territory, not Ohio."

"He joined up with Hale in Dodge City. He killed a man there in a fight over a woman," Johnson said, irritated at being interrupted. "To continue, these Ohio people just got tired of being flooded out every few years and losing about all they had, so they came up with the idea of organizing a sort of club—a grange, some called it.

"The plan was for each to save all the money they could for five years, then send someone they could trust with it to New Mexico or Texas, or maybe Arizona, where they wouldn't lose all they had every few years, and buy land they could settle on.

"There are thirty-eight families in the group and each came up with a thousand dollars over a period of seven years—five wasn't long enough since the river again got out of its banks during the time and set everybody back a bit."

"So this Adam Hale headed this was to buy land. Where does the sheriff come in?" Henry Tubbs wanted to know.

"I'm not sure how they got together," Johnson replied.

Preston, features dark, eyes filled with anger, said: "Why not let Tabor explain that?"

Riley, sensing the hostility that was now evident in the banker and the other men he considered his friends, shrugged.

"Why not? I met Hale in Dodge. He was in a fight with three men in a hotel there. I stepped in, helped him out. Afterwards he invited me to ride with him—said he was headed for New Mexico. I was looking for a ride—I'd just finished helping with a cattle drive to Dodge, and being afoot, took him up on his offer."

"We drove the Trail together—seems he'd lost the man who'd started out with him somewhere back up the line when they were fording a river."

"He wrote back about that," Johnson said.

"Anyway, that's what Hale told me. We took the Mountain Trail, and it was while we were going through Raton Pass that he decided to make it to the next town, Willow Springs, in a big hurry. The wagon turned over on a sharp curve and he was killed."

"That's where I picked up his trail—the grave alongside the road. Found out in that town that you had gone on in his wagon with a rancher named McKenzie. Hunted them up, but all they could tell me was that you kept going—for Texas, they thought. Lost track of you there, but I was being paid to find out what had happened to Hale so I kept on looking, going to a lot of places where I thought you might have gone. Then one day I picked up a newspaper—the *Cimarron News*—in a hotel where I was staying.

"It had reprinted a story that the paper here had run on a man named Riley Tabor who had become the new sheriff. That was the same name as that of the man who had been with Hale when he was killed, and took over all of his belongings, including the thirty-seven thousand dollars he was carrying. I packed up and caught the next stagecoach to here."

"Hale have that much money on him?" Tubbs asked. "Seems like a lot of cash for a man to—"

"Wasn't on him," Riley cut in, not liking the sound of the phrase. "He had it in a false bottom of his trunk. I never found it first off; it was when I was looking through his things trying to learn where he was from and who his folks were so that I could notify them of his death."

"You saying you rode all the way from Dodge City with him and he never said who he was and where he was from?" Johnson said incredulously.

"Name's all he ever told me—and that he was coming west to invest in land. Adam was no hand to talk about himself—closemouthed, you might say."

Someone in the small crowd that had gathered laughed derisively. Ward Preston's taut features were filled with doubt and disbelief.

"Hard to believe he never mentioned Ohio. Wasn't he carrying a wallet or a billfold—something with papers on it? Never saw a man who didn't."

"He had one—a billfold. Saw him open it once or twice when he wanted money. It was stolen—taken off him by one of the men who helped drag him out from under the wagon."

Johnson shook his head slowly. "Story you're telling me

is hard to believe—but it doesn't matter now. Have you still got the thirty-seven thousand dollars and Hale's team and wagon?"

"He put the money in my bank—let me think it was his!" Preston shouted angrily. "But those Ohio folks won't lose out. I invested most of it for him—good investments that are worth more now than they were at the start." The banker paused, and shaking his finger at Riley continued. "You fooled me right along—and you wormed your way into my family! I'll never—"

"Ease off a mite, Ward," Frank Brock said. "Riley told us he didn't know who to return that money to, and I believe him. Hell, he didn't blow it bucking the tiger in some saloon. And you said yourself those Ohio people will end up with more than they started with."

"Only because I took charge of it," Preston declared. "It was stealing as far as he's concerned—he's no better than a common thief!"

Riley glanced about at the gathering on the sidewalk, all taking in each word. He could have said that Adam Hale had told him before he died to take the money and invest it, that somebody would show up one day to claim it—but he didn't. Tabor was not the kind of man to lie even when he knew it would benefit him.

"I'm telling you this!" Preston said, again shaking his finger in Riley's face. "You forget about Rowena, about ever marrying her! I won't have a thief like you in my family!"

"I'll leave that up to Rowena," Riley said calmly, and turned to Johnson. "I used most of the money to make investments—a ranch, some land, and a building here in town and the like. Preston there handled it all and will have the records."

"All going to tally up to a damn sight more than the thirty-seven thousand you're after," Henry Tubbs observed.

"No doubt, and that's fortunate," Johnson agreed, "but it doesn't alter the fact the man took the money unlawfully. If I hadn't accidentally come across that newspaper article, like as not he would have used the money as his own forever."

"Absolutely right!" Preston said. Ward had settled down to some degree, although his eyes still glowed and his skin was flushed with anger. "If you'll step over to my bank I'll give you a full accounting."

"Don't be forgetting Riley's got some money of his own," Tubbs pointed out. "He's been drawing a salary here as sheriff, and I think there were a couple of pretty substantial rewards he collected."

Johnson nodded. "Of course, that is all his. And I expect my clients would not consider it unreasonable if I paid him a commission of sorts for his efforts."

"That mean you don't aim to prosecute?" Brock asked quickly.

Johnson stared out over the heads of the bystanders to the street. "I'm inclined not to. While I can't condone what he did, and his story of what happened isn't believable, I think the folks back in Ohio—considering what they've gained—will overlook any legal action."

"Only right they should," Tubbs declared, "and they ought to pay him—"

"I don't want anything but what I've earned," Riley cut in. "It's all yours. I'll sign quitclaim deeds for everything that I've got my name on. Just bring the papers over to my room at the hotel."

"I'll have them made up first thing," Johnson said.

"The sooner the better I'll like it," Tabor said, unpinning

his star and handing it to Brock. "I'll be leaving before dark." He hesitated, "Like to make one deal with you. My team and buggy in a swap for Hale's team and wagon."

Johnson frowned. "Hale was allowed a thousand dollars to buy that outfit. You figure yours is worth that much?"

"What if it ain't?" Henry Tubbs demanded. "Still be only fair for you to trade. Still say you owe him."

Johnson nodded. "All right, we have a deal. I'll bring the bills of sale over with the deeds." He turned to Preston. "I suppose we can have all the papers ready by noon?"

"We will," the banker said, and once more turned on Tabor. "Said you were leaving town today. Good. That's what we want. You flim-flammed all of us, including my daughter. Now, I don't want you trying to see her!" he said, suddenly angry again and shaking his finger in Tabor's face. "She'll get an explanation from me! I won't have you ly-ing—"

Temper at Ward Preston's attitude finally got the best of Tabor. He lashed out, knocked the banker's hand aside. A hard grin was on his face. Preston had once made it a point to call him "son," to talk confidently about the future, about their mutual plans. That had all vanished like a puff of smoke in the wind when the source of the money he had deposited had come to light. To the banker, no doubt fearful of what effect the incident might have on his political aspi-rations, Riley was someone to be publicly condemned and shunned. Regardless of what others thought, he'd had no choice but to do as he had done—and on that he would stand.

"I'll see Rowena when I please," he said in a low, hard voice, and turned away.

"Now wait a minute," Brock said hurriedly, stopping

him. "No need for you to leave town. Can't see any reason why you can't go on being sheriff."

Riley smiled tightly and glanced about at the faces staring at him from the doorway. Where once there had been friendliness he now saw only animosity.

"And have folks saying the town had a thief for a lawman? Obliged, Frank, but I couldn't do that to you."

By early afternoon Riley Tabor had said his few farewells in town, ridden the sorrel to the ranch and there packed the wagon while Caleb Ferrel hitched up the bay team. He was now aboard and ready to pull out.

"Been a pleasure knowing you," the old foreman said, shaking Riley's hand. "Mighty sorry you're leaving."

"Same here. Good luck," Riley replied, and swinging the rig about headed back toward the river.

Despite Ward Preston's warning he felt he must see Rowena. Perhaps if he explained it all to her she would see that there had been nothing else he could do, that he actually had not been dishonest. He had followed the only course that had been open—and it had all kicked back on him.

What was that verse in the Bible about a man not building his house on sand? He reckoned that was just what he had done—built his empire, as Ward Preston had termed it, on a false foundation, and it had collapsed. He'd had everything going for him for a while, although at times he'd felt a twinge of uncertainty as to how he had come by the money. But always the question had come to mind: What else could I have done with it? Entrusting Adam Hale's money to some stranger or to the army would have been foolish—and risky, as John McKenzie had pointed out. No, he had done what he had thought was right.

Rowena wasn't home, nor was her mother. The only person there was Rosa, the Mexican cook. Ward must have warned them to either stay out of sight or be absent at a neighbor's should he come calling.

"Por donde va ustéd?" Rosa asked as he dejectedly took up the lines and prepared to drive on.

Maybe it was just as well he didn't see Rowena. Parting would be difficult for both of them, and he was reluctant to be the cause of any trouble between the girl and her father.

"Oeste . . . Por Arizona—California—Oregon—quién sabe?" Riley replied with a shrug, and then added: *"Adiós, señora."*

"Adiós y buena suerte," Rosa murmured, and turned back into the house.

Lifting his hand, Riley, spirits low, his world in shambles about him, drove out of the Preston yard and pointing the bays south so as to avoid the town, reached the road that led westward and swung onto it.

He had no plans except to keep moving, to put the fine new life, and the love for the only woman who had ever come to mean anything to him, in the past. As he had told Rosa, he knew only that he was heading west; where he would eventually end up only time and miles would tell.

The road, paralleling the river flowing flat and silvery at a lazy pace, was well traveled, and the bays covered it with ease. The land was mostly flat, with bunch grass, low brush and an occasional yucca to be seen. Trees grew along the Feever, and the familiar whistle of a chevron-breasted meadowlark could be heard. The sky overhead was a clean, brilliant blue with no threat of rain.

Twisting about, intending to have his last look at the town where he'd had his first taste of importance and found the love of a beautiful woman, he frowned. A buggy was following—coming up fast. Riley studied it briefly and settled back: it was the rig he had traded to Johnson for Hale's team and wagon. Evidently the Ohio lawyer had something for him to sign, something he had missed earlier.

Shortly he was aware of the rig drawing up beside him. The horses were foaming with sweat, and dust rolled out from beneath the wheels of the buggy.

"Riley!"

Tabor came about swiftly on the seat. The voice was that of Rowena. Instantly he hauled back on the lines and brought the team to a stop. Rowena was out of the buggy quickly and hurrying toward him.

"What—" he began as he swung down from the wagon.

"Don't talk!" the girl said, throwing her arms about him, and then, in a voice taking on mock severity, added: "If you think you're going to get away from me this easy, Riley Tabor, you're badly mistaken! Hereafter, where you go—I go!"

"But your Pa—the trouble I'm in—"

"Trouble—fiddlesticks! And far as Pa's concerned, it's my life, not his. Soon as I found out what had happened and got the story from Frank Brock, I went looking for you. Rosa told me you'd already gone. I hurried then to the livery stable and persuaded Mr. Donovan to take me to you." Rowena paused, looked anxiously into his hard-planed face. "You are pleased, aren't you?"

"More than I can ever say," Riley replied, holding her close—and nodding his thanks to the stableman who was placing her suitcase in the wagon, added, "Come on, let's climb aboard. We've got a long way to go—and a lot of plans to make."